The Islam
Conspiracy

Matthias Richter

The Islam
Conspiracy

***Bibliografische Information der Deutschen Natio-
nalbibliothek:***
*Die Deutsche Nationalbibliothek verzeichnet diese
Publikation in der Deutschen Nationalbibliografie;
detaillierte bibliografische Daten sind im Internet
über http://dnb.dnb.de abrufbar.*

*TWENTYSIX - Der Self-Publishing-Verlag
Eine Kooperation zwischen der Verlagsgruppe
Random House und BoD-Books on Demand*

*© 2013 Matthias Richter
Herstellung und Verlag: BoD – Books on Demand,
Norderstedt*

ISBN: 978-3-7407-3474-9

Foreword

The so called Islamic State, which initially overran the middle east like a wave seems now to be on the decline and losing its caliphate. The Perschmerga played a vital role in the defeat of ISIS demanding a just compensation in form of an independent Kurdistan. But how could these young jihadi fighters hold up so long against multiple and highly trained armies?

As disclosed in the DIA Report of the pentagon of 2012, the US had knowledge that al Quaida was leading the opposition against Basar al Assad and that their goal was a caliphate of salafist shaping. The document also reveals that the »west« supported the opposition against Assad. But of course they only supported the moderate opposition...

Only an ingenuous person can believe that there is a moderate opposition in a war. The FSA has also chopped off heads of their captured enemies. And why shouldn't in this particular conflict the old proverb be valid: The enemy of my enemy is my friend?

Remember back when the US supported al Quaida against the Russian occupation in Afghanistan? The same elements of the deep state now used the jihadists against their new target, i.e. president Asad. Like in Afghanistan, Iraq and Lybia they did so accepting the predictable consequences of deaths, mass suffering and the refugee crisis.

Reality is wrong. Drams are real.
Tupac Shakur

Believe nothing
no matter where you read it
or who has said it, not even if I have said it
unless it agrees with your own reason
and your own common sense
Buddha

Love comes naturally, hate is learned
unknown

Chapter 1

Boba Fett stepped to the counter of the cinema on sunset Drive and picked up the tickets. The Star Wars Fans were anxiously awaiting the remake of the famous trilogy. Like most of the fans who didn't have VIP tickets, Andrew had spent the night waiting in line in front of the cinema. But he didn't mind as he did it for his princess Lea. »Did I promise too much?« He proudly gestured towards the crowd. The reception hall resembled a carnival Party. Stormtroopers, Jawas and Chewbaccas were bustling about to get some snacks and make it to their seats in time. »It should be illegal to call something a snack, which costs 18,50,- $!«, Andrew complained. »You are Crazy!« Sandy laughed and gave him a friendly pat on the shoulder. They went to the same class in the Miami High School. Sandy liked his smart and insightful character, which was different from most people she knew. She liked his kind of humor as well as their profound conversations which she could only have with him. Notwithstanding the cliche their fellow students gave them - ,the Beauty and the Beast' - they soon came to be close friends. Armed with their snacks they hurried to their seats. Luckily Andrew had managed to get Category A tickets, which meant quite central in the back. That way they didn't need to stretch their necks. »Did you switch off your phone?«, he asked Sandy cautiously. »It's starting.«

The people's eyes and mouths were wide open when the movie began and nobody dared to rustle with Pop Corn nor slurp on their Cokes. But there is always one idiot exception. Andrew cursed unbelievingly when his neighbor's smart phone vibrated and flashed up. »What is wrong with these people?«, he muttered. The man was even so bold and stood up and made his way through the aisle, disturbing all the other people. He didn't go to the toilets to take a call like everybody else, but walked all the way down to the emergency exit. Andrew was so irritated that he followed the guy with his eyes until he slipped through the emergency door. »What a jerk!«

Some moments later the door opened again and let the lighting through. »Of course! Here we go again!« The guy looked different though and his movements were also different. Things happened so fast. He made three steps to the center of the screen. Then he threw a smoke grenade into the hall yelling »Allahu Akbar!«, and started shooting indiscriminately into the crowd. An inferno erupted. Screams, panic and blood. Total chaos. Andrew was paralyzed. He clutched to the thought that it was all part of the show of the cinema. But then he saw a little girl being shot in the stomach and thrown back against the seats. Blood splashed in all directions. Real blood. And real fear. In the meantime the lights were switched on and a voice was heard through the speakers. »Homicide in Theater One. Homicide in Theater One!« Andrew grabbed Sandy and shook her. »Let's get out of here! Fast!« They climbed over the rows of seats and ducked down as soon as they reached the alley. Still more shots were bursting through the air. Andrew didn't know where they were coming from. So he kept down. At the exit people were jostling but Andrew didn't let go of Sandy's hand. When they finally reached the door, he looked back into the hall a last time. In a split second he became aware of corpses in unnatural positions. Bleeding, panicking faces contorted with pain and fear. The image burnt itself into his memory. In the reception hall police men and black clad men from a special unit kept running in the direction of Theater One. In the background sirens were howling. And the flashing police and ambulance lights everywhere. The cinema had changed into a crime scene. Exhausted and drained they sat down on the stairs. »Did you see that?«, Sandy whimpered drenched in tears. »The little girl was shot in the chest and in the head! And all the blood.« She broke into tears and Andrew was about to give in to tears as well. Instead he stroked her hair. »It's alright. It's gonna be fine.« He knew that his words sounded hollow in the face of death, but he couldn't think of anything else to say. So he kept hugging and comforting Sandy as good as possible. Without entirely grasping what had been going on, they watched the ambulance taking care of injured people, parents who cried over their dead children and children who cried over their dead parents.

Chapter 2

At ten o'clock sharp the display of his phone illuminated and smooth hinduistic tunes filled his room and invited him with a happy *Namaste* to a new day. The shutters opened automatically and gave sight to the bright and trickling sun beams. The kind of energy boost he needed to get out of bed. Usually. But this night had been a nightmare for Chris. He had laid sleeplessly and pondered over one single thought in his mind: »Was it the right decision? Should I really pull it off?« But he knew he couldn't pull out at the last moment.

After his studies of journalism the young man from Berlin had some problems starting off and finding a job. After one year of sending out dozens and dozens of applications he got somewhat disillusioned. His parents slowly started to withdraw their financial support and Chris was forced to work as a personal trainer again. His dream as a successful journalist was not even in sight and he grew more and more anxious. He needed a sensational story that the media outlets couldn't ignore. And he was on the edge and willing to do everything for that story.

He became a regular at the exclusive restaurant Borchardt's, where politicians used to meet and tried to make connections. After a short while he befriended a young politician from the green Party, who was working in a commission on the Islamic State. She liked the young and hungry journalist and wanted to help him. »Whenever there is a kidnapping by a terror organization the German government uses so called Jumpers. These Jumpers are supposed to make contact with the terrorist group and settle a ransom«, she told him over a glass of wine. »That is of course, only after all the other actions and possibilities to free the citizen are too risky or infeasible.« Chris swallowed her words. She also told him it was planned to send a Jumper to Syria and Iraq in order to free a German Citizen. »The Jumper is an experienced undercover agent called Paulsen.« She looked Chris in the eyes. »If you are willing to go... I could arrange for you to accompany him?« Chris' eyes were beaming and he confirmed that he was committed to go.

He had had many encounters with politicians that promised a lot but didn't execute. But this time it was different. After only 2 days he had received a short and poignant email by Paulsen: »Let's meet!«

And the next day they sat at a table in a little pub. After having scrutinized Chris thoroughly, Paulsen began. »You want a big story, eh? Well, you can have it. You might know, that the Islamic State had brutally murdered two Journalists this year. These graphic videos went viral and were a huge propaganda success for the Jihadists. Now another journalist is exposed and is waiting the death penalty. We need to avoid another propaganda video. So we pay them. Can you follow?« Chris nodded slightly. »We've planned for some time to bring a person to the Heart of the Islamic State that

5

has an extra eye for detail and is able to report.« He glanced at Chris in an indiscriminate manner. Our common friend spoke highly of you. You must have been good in bed. Or whatever... she said you are brave and are quick on the uptake. I need someone like that. Are you hungry and fearless?« Chris returned his look and nodded his head. »Yes Sir, You came to the right person.«

Paulsen clapped his hands. »Fine, then I have company for the trip to the Caliphate.«

At 6 p.m. the Maerst Alabama was landing in King Fahad Industrial Port Yanbu. Miller was standing at the rail and smoking a cigarette. He had joined the container ship by helicopter this morning. With top-class clients it was usual practice of the company for the vendor to supervise the shipment and attend the delivery. As an extra service. Even though Miller had done this numerous times before he was equally stunned by the 155m x 25m container ship. A town on the water. When the ship was anchored and he stepped on the port, he was greeted by his business partner *Sheikh* al-Walid and his entourage. They knew each other for a long time and they respected and trusted each other. »Welcome to the Arabic Peninsula, my American friend.« He reached out for his hand and shook it. »Delighted to meet you, too.« Miller responded in the same light hearted manner. The *Sheikh* glimpsed over his shoulder towards the containeship. »Did you bring my new little toys?« Miller gave in to a grin.

»Yes, it is top-notch quality. I am sure, you will love 'em.«

Chris was seated in the economy class of Turkish Airways and looked into the clouds pondering over his mission. The phenomenon and the rise of the Islamic State to a global threat had shocked the whole world. Nobody had deemed it possible for the off-shoot of Al Qaida, with its origins in the wake of the Arabic Spring in Syria, to conquer so much land in such a short period of time and keep it. The shock gave in to the realization that the Islamic State had changed from a terror group into an established state. What the Jihadists lacked in military training, they made up with their incomparable religious zeal. They longed for death in combat for that would bring them directly to paradise. Chris remembered a story of the crash course he was given, which dealt with an old islamic fighter whose whole body was spangled with scars. He had only one single goal. To die for Allah. But he survived again and again. When he lay in his death bed, he despondently mourned over the fact that he never received the honor of dying as a martyr.

This zeal was revived by the young men of the Islamic state. This made it possible for them to compete and to win against much larger armies in the region. Thus within a few years they had managed to change the map in the middle east drastically. »Chili con carne or Pasta, Sir?« The voice of the stewardess of Turkish Airlines brought Chris back to reality. A tall and beautiful woman with black long hair was smiling at him. Chris regained his composure. »Chili con Carne in an airplane with over 200 passengers? What terrorist came up with this menu?« He winked at her and she smiled back. »Sir, at least you are seated at the emergency exit, so you might have a chance to escape.«

After lunch Chris fell asleep and was only awakened by the pilot's landing speech.

Konstantinopel! Chris had to think of the capital of the Byzantine Empire. A mega city with over 12 million inhabitants stretched before his eyes. An endless net of houses and streets, even from above. At the same time it was the frontline to the adjacent Islamic State who had started firing against their neighbor.

Chris met his companion Paulsen in the lobby of the Four Seasons in the center of Istanbul. Paulsen had traveled there some days before to take some preperations. The two men that were from now on dependent on each other, greeted themselves with a glass of Jack Daniels. »At least you no longer look like a fashion victim.« Paulsen stated in his dry manner. Chris had grown his beard long and thick which gave him - in accordance with his dark tan - an orientalic note. He had noticed before that the taxi driver had talked to him in Turkish. Paulsen in contrast was rather pale and skinny. But you could see from his face that he had some tremendous life experience. Other than that he emanated a

8

kind of sovereignty that was palatable in the whole room. »As we don't want anybody to know what we're doing - especially not the Turkish - we take the same route as the Jihadists. With the help of traffickers«, he continued explaining. »First we go to Gaziantep. There we stay alert until they call us.« He took the glass and emptied it. »After that there is no way back.«

»Darth Vader attacks!«, read the headline of the Miami Herald. Adriana Borrero sat at the breakfast table and read the article carefully. The whole weekend there was no other talk in town. In the media, in the living rooms and in the streets. People could not grasp what had happened. Again. They showed their compassion for the relatives of the victims and anger against the perpetrator. Within 10 months it was the 3rd religiously motivated attack. And this was by far the most deadliest.

Adriana slowly repeated the numbers that every person in Miami knew by now: 17 dead people, 4 gravely injured and 21 injured. For that reason they called him the Black Jack killer. Adriana's son Santo started whining and she took him out of his seat and onto her lap. »Ven mi hijo, the mush is so yummy, Sabroso. She took a spoon and ate it with pretended pleasure. The single mum was a court psychiatrist and her job was to render an expert opinion on murder cases. They had informed her that her next client was the very Black

Jack, the whole city was talking about. She had had several murderers in her practice in the City Jail but it was the first time she had a mass murderer of this category. For that reason she felt an undefined unease. Her mother came down the stairs and joined them at the breakfast table. »Buenos dias, mi hija y mi corazon.« She gave each of them a kiss and sat down. After having finished, they got ready to leave. It was a daily routine in the Borrero family. Her mother drove Adriana to work, brought Santo to the kindergarten and went to the grocery store. »Que terrible es?« Her mother began while wheeling the car out of the gateway. »So many dead and wounded by this Black Jack. »Se ha vuelto muy peligroso por aca. We live in dangerous times, mi hija.« Adriana knew that a rant was on the way, but she had no means of stopping her mum. »You should send these Muslims to jail right away. You are not safe anymore anywhere. I mean, it can happen in the supermarket, in the subway, in the streets - se puede pasar for doquier!« Adriana nodded. Her mum gave the same speech as after the past attack. The first time it happened she was so intimidated that she refused to leave the house for 2 weeks. Now she somewhat got used to it. »But Mum, remember that your son Luis is also Muslim. Not all muslims are terrorists.« Adriana regretted having cut that topic right away. Her mother retorted furiously. »That is Luis! What an idiotic idea for a Cuban living in Miami to convert to Islam. He has got as little to do with Islam as with the Ku-Kux Clan. If he really wanted to discover his roots he should have found out more about the Santeria. The worship of the of the Saints, Santeria, was a common religious practice that was particularly famous in Cuba after the induction of freedom of religion. It had its origins in the slave communities in the 18. Century and was a mix between Catholicism and the beliefs of the kidnapped African slaves. »That's where he's coming from! But No. Luis has to be that obstinate child and do things completely different«, she complained. Adriana on the other hand couldn't stand it if her mother talked that way about her beloved brother. She had a special connection to him and they stuck together against all odds. »You must not criticize him for all he does. You know how he reacts to that. Try to understand him and he will open up to you more and more. You should know that by now.« She changed the subject. »Regarding the attack I will soon find out more about the motives of Black Jack.« Her mother shook her head. »And by the way, how is it possible that a young man can purchase rifles that easily? That should be forbidden at once.« That was the position of a growing number of people and politicians alike: They demanded the ban on guns. And with the growing number of attacks they had the momentum on their side. »Armas para que?« Her mother asked rhetorically. »For what young men need to have guns? If nobody has a gun you don't need to protect yourself from a gunman. In Cuba there is also a general ban on weapons. Not all Castro did was wrong. You know that.« Adriana was relieved when she saw the facade of the Jail Complex which contained her work place. She gave her son a kiss and left them to themselves.

Moments after she entered the Pre-Trial Detention Center. It contained 1712 beds for male inmates and belonged to the Miami renowned Dade County Corrections System. She sorted her files of Black Jack on her table and threw a reassuring glance at the wall behind her desk, where fotos and certificates as personal accessories and historic artifacts of healing were supposed to lend the place an personal and professional aura. Inconspicuous trustworthy. In the session the patients would sit in the fluffy couch in the center of the room, whose walls were painted orange. Because orange sent a relaxed and serene atmosphere. The last thing she had installed purposely were the many green plants. They were supposed to bring about the feeling of security, tranquility and comfort. The right thing for inmates who came out of their grey cells to feel comfortable.

In all her years Adriana had hosted some of the worst creatures in her cosy practice. Murderers, rapists, drug addicts, gangsters etc. And most of them had the same strategy, i.e. claiming to be not responsible for their actions because of insanity or substance abuse. So it was her job to find out who really had a condition that diminished or even excluded his capacity to discernment.

At 11 o'clock there was a knock on her door. »Hi Sam, Hi Carl.« Adriana greeted the officers who had brought the infamous Black Jack with them. The murderer wore a straitjacket with the sleeves tied together. He was pale like a sheet of paper and his face a display pure distress. Under his dark hair the meager young man looked at her with his gleaming eyes. The officers sat him down at the desk and left the room. When the door was shut, Adriana took a deep breath and opened her files. Yusuf Zaidi, 24 years old, native Maroccan, born in the US.«

Sheikh al-Walid had the delivered goods presented to him. On a secluded part of the port they were looking at three army all terrain vehicles of the brand Oshkosh, which he had purchased at an arms exhibition in Dubai. Miller explained the technical details and assets of the brand new product. The JLTV is a sequel to the M-ATV. It has a length of 6,30m and a weight of 11 tons.« They went around the vehicle. Its Caterpillar engine has a horsepower of 374, which equals a forward speed of 80 mph and a reverse speed of 8 mph. Miller saw that his friend was not so much interested in the details but rather in the armament. »The JLTV can carry various light and medium caliber weapons, plus AGLs or ATGWs if required and carries up to 4 smoke grenade dischargers. The sheik's expression lighted up. »That humvee is exactly what I was looking for.« He gave Miller a friendly pat on the shoulder and signaled his people to get the humvees out of the port. »I am pleased with your products as always.«

Chapter 3

The first breath of air on the airfield in Gaziantep didn't bode well. The smell of burnt material lingered in the air. When they left the airport the smell didn't vanish. »That is probably due to the cars without catalysator and the diesel generators«, the driver answered their question. Chris shrugged with his shoulder. But was as a bad omen. The region was barren and dreary and only once in a while animals appeared on the side of the road. Chris grew melancholic. »No wonder people here are getting creative with the goats.« Paulsen frowned his forehead and kept on studying his map. »Gaziantep is the capital of the province with the same name. It is 35 miles from the Syrian border. The traffickers work from here in order to avoid the police.« In the distance the City lights appeared. The contrast couldn't be more drastically. There were a few huge hotel complexes whose glaring lights bedazzled one's eyes. Apparently the city was attractive for the industry and the money. But the normal population lived in basic if not decrepit conditions. The city also had a bad rep for it was no secret that the Jihadists started their adventure from here. Accordingly Chris observed the people in the hotel lobby carefully and vice versa.

The next day the were up early and ready to go, but there was no call from their contact. They waited until lunchtime and then decided to go to the old city. In the market Chris felt like he had time-traveled to medieval times. There was a fuss of voices, honking and hammering. They stopped to watch a man hammer an embellishment into a brass plate. »This is art!« Chris was also impressed by the wide offer of nuts on every corner. As recent vegetarian he liked to have his proteins from nuts. For a small change he mixed a big bag of Cashews, Pekan, Pistaccios and sultanas. He was in good temper when they returned to the hotel and he went straight to the Hamam. »What a nice trip so far! And the best thing is that the German government pays for it!« He was still heated in his face when he met Paulsen in the lobby that evening. Paulsen looked at him and frowned. »You might think we are on our honeymoon. But we are not.« He patted Chris hard on his shoulder. »We have to adjust to the local food so we won't crap our pants when we cross the border.«

They drove to the oldest Kebab house in town and ordered Shish-Kebab. It was served with a side salad, fresh pita bread, a bowl of humus, spicy chilis and grilled kebab. It was delicious. Chris tried to stay away from the meat at first, but then silently decided that it was not feasible to remain vegetarian on this mission. So he gladly changed his status to meat lover. He also eased his mind with the knowledge thatthese animals didn't come from industrial cattle breeding but were rather treated like family members.

Paulsen couldn't refrain from laughing. »You know what a flexitarian is?« Chris shook his head as he was chewing the succulent meat. »Somebody told me recently. It's those part-time vegetarians who can't fully relinquish eating meat and then have to ease their conscience like you just did.«

Chris joined in the laughter. Paulsen became more and more talkative and almost likable. He told Chris about his recent mission with the Pakistani Taliban were he negotiated the release of 5 German charity workers. »I had worked with the same Taliban commander for years and it was almost a friendly cooperation. They were rational and you could rely on their word because they really only wanted the ransom.« He sipped on his tea. »It's a different thing with the Islamic State. It is the first mission and we were negotiating for almost half a year. Yet, we don't have trusted contacts and they are unpredictable. They assured us our safety, but you know... the first mission is always a risky one.« He reached in his jacked and pulled out a piece of paper. »This is your safety guarantee signed by the official office of the Kalif Abu Bakr al Bagdadi.« On the paper were some Arabic words and a stamp. Chris was puzzled and Paulsen explained. »It says that they guarantee our personal safety and that of our belongings. Signed by the bureau of the caliph.« Chris frowned. »By his Bureau? Is there a reason why he couldn't sign it himself? That would have been more reassuring.« He folded the paper and put it into his trousers. »The self proclaimed Caliph Abu Bakr al Bagdadi has only once appeared publicly, and that was in Raqqa in 2013, when he proclaimed the Caliphate of the Islamic State. But the Services are convinced that he exists and is running the business in the background, unlike Osama bin Laden. So yeah, I think we can trust it«, Paulsen explained. »But you have to be aware of the fact, that as soon as we are in their so called Caliphate, we have other threats to worry about. It is a secret mission. Nobody knows who we are there. So the coalition will continue to drop bombs and shoot rockets from the sky. It can hit in any market or places we go. Especially as we will meet the leading figures of the Islamic State.« He casually waved the waiter for the check. »I didn't want to worry you... but just to let you know what you are in for, right?«

Back in the hotel Chris did worry over the words of his friend. He switched on the TV and zapped around until he ended up with CNN. They had the latest news on Syria and Iraq and showed a devastated house with crying people shouting in the cameras. »In the last week 40 civilians died in Iraq at the hands of the Coalition. Only in this month American airstrikes had caused more than 110 dead, although but the number is not verified.« Chris shut off the TV. That was no distraction at all. He thought of his family and pictured how they would react in case he wouldn't return. He choked. Was it worth worth it? He thought about dumping the whole thing. But he knew he would never ever be able to look in the mirror, in case he missed this great opportunity to come up with a great story. He remembered that he had another episode of his favorite Show on his lap-top called ‚The Newsroom'. He watched it until he fell as-leep.

The next day he woke up with major diarrhea and hastened to the toilet. It had become true of what Paulsen had warned him of. The bacteria were different than back home. Chris dropped his plans of going to the hamam early and instead stayed exactly where he was. At the loo. He hoped that their contact wouldn't call them today. And he was lucky. No pho-ne call that day.

Chris took some medicine and was getting better. But Paul-sen grew more and more nervous waiting for the call. When they strolled the market the next day his smartphone finally rang. The caller told them to be ready the next day. He even apologized for the delay. »You know, we are in a war right now. That's why things are sometimes unpredictable.«

Paulsen introduced Chris for the first time as his fellow ne-gotiator and the man at the other end who called himself Abu Masala had no objections.

Chapter 4

Mr. Zaidi, I want you to know that everything we discuss, every detail you mention within these orange walls, is 100% confidential and will not be used against you. I am exclusively interested to figure out if you are culpable or not. All other incriminating information can not be used in court«, Adriana began her standard introduction. Zaidi had a confused look on his face, but nodded slightly. »Do you feel like talking to me right now?« Zaidi nodded again. She noted that he was tired and exhausted, but his eyes were wide open and his pupils big like marbles. He looked like a hunted down animal. »Tell me about your last two days here. Could you find some sleep?« Zaidi wanted to make a gesture with his hands but instantly realized that he was in a straitjacket. »I have tremendous panic attacks. And I hear voices. Even if there is nobody in my room«, he let Adriana know with a soft voice. He scanned the room again and continued. »The first 24 hours were hard. Now I feel a little better.«

»You are now in solitary confinement. Could you find some sleep?« Adriana made a note and repeated her question. »I don't do anything else. I feel fatigue like I never had before in my entire life. But maybe that's normal after what has happened.« »That is normal. The new impressions, the new environment. The new food. All that has to be processed. But the good thing is, humans are good at adjusting to new conditions. It will be better«, she reassured him. During their small talk Adriana observed that her patient still exhibited an unusual great extend of confusion. But she figured he was ready for the screening method. That was a method to study the eye movement. As the brain has different compartments like imagination, remembrance and so on, the eyes will correspondingly look in a certain angle. You could elaborate a pattern with the information you had and then work with this pattern. If you got aberrations you had a clue that something was odd. Probably the subject was lying. So she took the folder and started off with some factual questions. Please answer with ‚Yes' or ‚No'. »Your name is Yusuf Zaidi. »Yes.« »You were born on the 3rd of march in 1993 in Miami.« »Yes«. You studied neuro sciences at Miami State University and graduated ‚cum laude'. »Yes.« »You are Muslim.« Zaidi paused for a moment. Adriana paused surprised. Zaidi held up his digit and shot back. »There is no god but god. And Mohamed is his messenger! Islam is the only religion, the way the Caliph has taught us.« Adriana took notes. »So I suppose they already questioned you. Do you know what you are accused of? Did you talk to them?« Zaidi looked gloomily out of the window. »What is there else to say? It's all in the video tapes.« »Did you confess?« She asked although she knew the answer from her files. Zaidi nodded. »Then I assume you are you willing to talk about what happened that night in the cinema. I would like to know about your motive of killing those people. Do you want to tell me about it?« Zaidi clenched his fist visibly under the straitjacket. »All enemies of Allah have to die. That is our obligation as devout muslims«, he retorted angrily. Adriana was surprised by the new change of attitude. »Would you like to tell me about the night? How did you do it?« Zaidi seemed annoyed but was willing to talk. »I sneaked out of the cinema, went to my car and got my AK47, then I went back and did what I had to do. How my Emir has ordered us to deal with the Kufar.« Adtriana met his eyes. »One last question. Can you tell me where you got the weapon from?« »No I can't, because that whole thing here is ridiculous.« He gazed out the window and made clear that the conversation was ended. But Adriana couldn't let him make the rules. So they sat 15 more minutes in silence while she went through his files. When the time was over she opened the door and dismissed Zaidi. She had mixed feelings as she watched him being taken back to his cell.

A culpable mental state is a necessary element of every crime. In order to be convicted of a particular crime, there must be proof that the actor possessed the requisite state of mind when the crime was committed.

Adriana knew the definition by heart and kept thinking about Zaidi as she was playing with her son in his room. He sat on his favorite toy which was a rocking horse that Adriana got hold of at a flea market. Her brother had painted it blue and it looked like new. Santo chuckled happily as Adriana gave him a little push. He had the same blue eyes as his father Jason had. The thought of Jason still brought tears to her eyes. She wanted to be strong and move on with her life but it was so difficult to forget the man she had loved so much. But she also wanted to be strong for Santo, for she knew how important it was for a child to have a father figure. Her brother was the best example of a kid who grew up without a father. Her mother could not control him and save him from the many bad influences. She wanted that to be different with Santo. And she wanted to have a real family. She sighed. Then she took up the phone and messaged her brother. »Hey Luis. How are you? I would like to come visit you next week. Tidy up your room, when I come. Hug.«

Paulsen and Chris sat in the lobby waiting for the journey to begin. Chris drank a whiskey straight and smoked a last ci-cigarette. Also Paulsen was cracking his knuckles nervously. Then suddenly the phone rang. They were instructed to take a taxi and pass the smartphone over to the driver. He would given the exact direction. They did so and the driver headed out of town for about 15 minutes. Then they stopped next to a mini van. They paid and the new driver of the van rushed them inside. They were greeted by three young men who according to the smell of old sweat had been driving for quite a while. But they were good-humored and smiled happily. After all they were all ‚brothers‘. Chris took some notes of their appearance. The young men wore track pants with undershirts and worn shoes. Their faces looked robust. Chris guessed they were from the countryside. The nose of one guy was so badly crooked that he was forced to stare at it like people watching an accident. On inquiry he learnt that one guy was from Aserbaidschan and the other two from Kasachstan and that they were between 23 and 27 years old. They were the kind of people who had nothing to lose by joining the Islamic State. For them it rather meant a new chance. Fighters could earn a decent amount of money and apart from that they were entitled to take sex slaves, which might have been equally appealing for these men. The van stopped and another person joined them. Chris was surprised to learn that the young woman was a 35 year old German from Berlin. Her reason to join the IS, he learnt, had been the fact that the authorities had taken away her child after her journey to Mekka, without any other reason. Pure discrimination. So she now wanted to live in a place where she could live her religion. Chris noted that she also belonged to the category of the disappointed. The young men were obviously nervous. While Chris was talking in the back with the Berlin woman, the guy from Aserbaidschan suddenly interrupted him agitatedly. »Are you intelligence? Or journalist?« Chris tried to ease the tension by cracking a joke. »Yes I am intelligent, why? You're not?« That joke was not received well and caused more agitation. Paulsen threw him an angry look whispering. »Well done! Now they think we are intelligence

23

or reporters. You know what they do with these people.« One of the men made the scythe gesture and let it be known that they would take things into their hands after they crossed the border. Chris grew nervous and urged Paulsen to call the contact and settle the issue before they reached the border. Paulsen agreed and called his number. He passed the phone to the guy from Aserbaidschan and after some words he seemed to understand that the Germans were welcome and important guests in the Caliphate. After hanging up he explained the situation to his brothers and they instantly relaxed and seemed relieved. Chris also took a deep breath. That was a clumsy start. Paulsen explained to him that the Turkish authorities would send them to prison for trying to join the Islamic State. For that reason they were so anxious. The shuttle stopped near a playground and they switched and got into two taxis. In their taxi there were 2 old Arabic men, so that they had to squeeze in 4 people in the back. With the 2 packed taxis they looked like a Turkish family on the move. It was not exactly inconspicuous. The taxi driver was a young Turkish with oily hair and a cool leather jacket. He apparently earned good money on the side with the trips to the Islamic State. But he looked nervous as well. They drove in the direction of the Syrian border. The landscape became dry and barren again and less populated. Suddenly the two taxis left the main road and sped across country towards the border. It was almost funny if it weren't that dangerous. After their rally they reached a place that was protected from sight by a bunch of trees. From there you could see the Turkish border tower who looked on the barren ground like a lighthouse. Almost impossible to cross the area with 12 men without being spotted. But just that was the plan. »Yalla, Yalla!« The traffickers shouted and signaled them to run the distance over the field. Chris grabbed his suitcase and chased after the trafficker in a ducked down position. They crossed a barb wired fence with a hole inside and kept running towards another group of trees, in about 250 meters distance. When he looked over his shoulder for Paulsen, he realized that the rest of the group was not as fast on their feet. The three men were shortly behind him breathing heavily under their luggage. Behind them Paulsen and the woman walking fast. And behind them the old Arabic men strolling casually like they were on a bazaar. Chris reached the trees where some cars were parked and new drivers waited for the newcomers. When everybody had reached the cars, they hugged and congratulated each other happily with AllahuAkbar shouts. The young man with the scythe gesture shook hands with Chris and excused himself for his malbehaviour. Then one of the new drivers stepped in front of the group and read out the names asigning them their respective cars. When Chris and Paulsen were seated in a car, they changed a quick look, that said: »We have entered the cave of the lion.«

Chapter 5

Adriana had left Santo with her mother and met her former colleague Emanuel Ortega for a walk at the beach on this sunny Saturday afternoon. Ortega was police officer in the murder squad of the Miami Police department and a friend of her late husband. Especially after her husband's death he had become a dear friend to Adriana and maybe even more than that. »Shoot. What's your first impression of Black Jack?« Ortega wanted to know right away, while they were walking on the beach. Before Adriana could answer, he added. »You know, I was one of the first officers on the ground at that night and I would have loved to investigate it. But they took it from us, just like that.« He snapped with his finger and sighed disappointedly. Adriana put her arm on his shoulder. »His name is Yusuf Zaidi. So far we only had one session and that was about 3 days after the massacre.« She recalled the interview. »You should have seen him. He was confused and showed no emotions initially. Like paralyzed. Without orientation.« Adriana stopped and watched into the turquoise sea. »And no history of schizophrenia... If I hadn't read the medical report, I would have guessed he was on heavy drugs like LSD.« She glanced at Ortega. »In the beginning he was tacit, his answers were brief and concise. He even had confessed earlier to the police. But then suddenly, when I asked about his motives he changed completely. He was so angry and shouted that all nonbelievers had to die and it was the obligation of every muslim to do so. And more scary was not what he said, but how he said it, with these glowing passionate eyes.« She looked puzzled. Ortega nodded his head. I know this behavior from other Jihadists. They regurgitate the same phrases over and over again. As if they all came from the same mosque. They are brainwashed.« Adriana thought about her friend's words. She took off her sandals and stepped into the warm water. Ortega was right. In order to determine an aberration you had to have a comparison group. That was psychology one on one. »Do you know a jihadist who is willing to talk to me?«, she asked. »Well, My Grandma is in town...« Adriana laughed and splashed some water in Ortega's direction. »But seriously, only last week we stopped a jihadist from joining the Islamic State. But he is waiting for his trial and he will probably not talk. I'll give you some names of prisoners of the Metro West on Monday.« Adriana thanked her friend and they kept moving. »Why did they take the case from you?«, she wanted to know. »It was really strange. We had started with our investigation. You know, asking witnesses, securing proof and samples from the scene, confiscating the video recordings, and all of that. But after only two days the FBI came in and took the case from us. They claimed it was a federal case because of the terror motive and they had information of further attacks. We offered them to work together or at least give them a briefing on our info we had. But they refused both. They wanted to do their own investigation. As if we were amateurs.« Ortega cursed angrily. They kept walking in silence. Adriana enjoyed these walks with her friend and wanted to perk him up. »You worked out a lot lately? 'cause you look quite massive.« She stroked his triceps with a grin on her face. »Yeah you might be right. I have been in the gym a lot lately. If you don't have a girl friend, you have too much time...« He grinned back at her and let his chest bounce. With the chiseled body and his sun glasses the native Argentinian looked like ‚the Rock'. With Adriana next to him they were the latin american version of Barbie and Kent. And they knew it. »Oh, I hope it's your cheat day today, because I want to have some ice cream with you.« She winked at him playfully. Ortega came close to her and whispered. »There is nothing more I would rather do at this moment.« Their lips came closer but a moment before they met, Adriana stepped back. Ortega bit his lip. »Adriana, you should know, whenever you - or your brother - need help, I'll be there for you. I promise.«

The sun had almost set, when Adriana went to visit her brother in Opa-locka. She loved her brother, but she hated Opalocka. It was an abbreviation for the Indian word Opatishawockalocka, which meant an area of raised land in a swamp. And a swamp it was indeed. Opa-locka was infested with crime and had one of the highest rate of violent crime in the

United States. It was on every list for tourists to stay away from. People were 7 times more likely to become victim of a crime than in other American cities. And it was also the place where her husband was shot point blank by a minor. He had been conducting a routine check in front of a liquor store and the young thug didn't like to be searched. So he shot him twice in the head. Over a bottle of Heineken and a small amount of weed. But her husband was gone forever. That was the moment when Adriana left Opa-locka with her mother.

She parked the car in front of her brother's apartment building in 2400 of Northwest 135th Street. Even the residents called this area a war zone. The triangle. Adriana was about to yell at the kids: Go home! It's too dangerous on the streets.« Statistically every week one child died on the streets here by random bullets.   But then again, where should the children play? She sighed and rang the bell. A moment later her brother opened the door and greeted her with a wide grin. Luis was a tall and slender Latino with full black hair. Once he was a handsome man every woman in the hood wanted to go out with. But age and drug abuse brought wrinkles to his haggard face and his once vivid eyes were now painted dark by the circles underneath. But Adriana loved her brother the way he was. »Mi Hermanito!« She jumped into his arms and received a warm hug. He invited her in and Adriana's enjoyment of reunion vanished slightly when she glanced at the sparse conditions her brother chose to live. The three rooms contained only the necessary items and her brother was not known for his tidiness. He clearly needed a woman in the house. »How are you holding up, Luis?« Adriana asked plaintively. He evaded her look. »Todo bien. You know how it is here. Keep hustling and doing whatever it takes to make your ends meet. But life goes on«, he assuaged her. Adriana didn't like it when he talked the ‚Triangle vernacular' to her. And he knew it. »You look tired.« »Yeah, there was a shooting one block away with wailing and police and ambulance and the whole crap. You know.« Adriana shook his head. »I cannot understand why on earth you don't want to come to us. We have a house with plenty of space and Santo and Mum would love to have you with us.« »Adriana, please. You bring it up every time and you know my answer is no. I can't live with mum. I will not be a burden to you and even though I'd love to see Santo more often I can't. I have to settle my issues by myself.« He pointed at his apartment. »I'm fine. I'm a grown up.« Adriana didn't want to disgruntle her brother so she gave in. »You only should know, that we would love to have you with us. And you can come whenever you change your mind about it. That's all.« She went to the fridge and opened the door. Three bottles of milk, cheese and yoghurt. It saddened her to see her brother live like this. She slammed the door a little to hard. »You should eat more. You look meager. Do you abuse again, Luis?« He evaded her look again and gazed out of the window. He was a bad liar. He was like the other kids in the hood. And she knew how difficult it was to grow up as a man in the hood. There was a lot of pressure and you were either a sheep or a wolf. Clearly nobody wanted to be a sheep. And in order to be a lion you had to earn your respect. And in the hood it were the bad things that earned you respect. She felt empathy with the boys and adolescents who grew up here. But she was also convinced that a man was responsible for his actions regardless of how bad his childhood was. And there came a time when every person had to decide on where his life was heading. And Luis took bad decisions by staying in this area. And it was getting worse every year. The gangs became more numerous and gang members younger. As a young court psychiatrist she had started off in Opa-locka. So she knew about the dead people every week over children's arguments, like a wrong look, a wrong word or just the wrong place ate the wrong time. That used to happen when children got hold of weapons. In this point she agreed with her mum. »By the way, mum sends you a big hug and Santo misses you too.«That instantly put a smile to Luis's face. She showed him some videos of her little son on her phone and told him about his achievements. Then she told him about her work, because she knew that her brother was proud of her. »You heard of Black Jack? You know who his court psychologist is?« He lit up even more. »My big sister? Really? That is - so exciting!« He exclaimed. The whole city is talking about the massacre. And also Opa-locka, of course. Adriana still felt the bond with Opa-locka, although she hated it, and was curious. »What they say in the Triangle about the case?« Luis shrugged his shoulder. »They say, things may not be like they seem. Thy say there are some things that don't add up. There is a rumor that it might be an inside job.« Adriana had to smirk. That was always the first guess in the Triangle. The police were hated and nobody trusted the authorities. »Oh that's an original thought. They both laughed and it felt so good. But her time was already over. »I have to return home and eat with Santo. I just wanted to see how you're doing.« She pulled three hundred dollars out of her pocket and lay it on the table. Luis had stopped trying to fend off the charity, because there was no point arguing. So he accepted the money. Adriana gave him a warm hug and headed back home.

Chapter 6

After a short while they reached a little village and the driver pulled into a gateway of a little house and got out of the car. Seconds later a masked man with a Kalashnikov appeared. »Are you Journalists?«, he asked fidgeting his weapon. Paulsen had anticipated the situation and had his contact on the phone who explained the guy that they were invited by the Caliph. The masked man immediately changed his tone and welcomed them to the Islamic State. Chris was relieved and pleased with the telephone joker. »Did you see the look on his face?«, Chris joked. »He was looking forward to have some journalists grilled.« He gradually gained confidence in the security guarantee. The driver returned and drove them to a nearby village into something like an arrival camp. They took off their shoes and passed an ante chamber where several stranded young men from all parts of the world prayed or talked quietly. A young black man with big sun glasses and colored blond hair attracted Chris' attention. He approached the Dennis Rodman character and greeted him. »Asalamalaikum, brother.« The flamboyant man told him he was Malik from Trinidad and Tobago. »Really?« Chris shouted out in surprise. »It's a beautiful island. For what reason did you leave Trinidad and Tobago, if I may ask?« »Too much promiscuity«, Malik shot back concisely. Chris knew what he meant. He was there on vacation the past summer and there were prostitutes all over the place. He didn't want to bother him any longer, though and said good-bye.

They were picked up and led in a back room where they were received by the supervisors of the camp. A Young Algerian and a young Syrian. Fortunately Paulsen spoke fluent French and could communicate who they were and who they wanted to meet. The Algerian was friendly and Chris sensed that he had real pity for the Non-belivers who would burn in hell. Without the security guarantee he might not have had that sympathy. While Paulsen talked with them in French, Chris took a look around the room. A big blackboard at the wall caught his eye. »This was a school once.« Without having noticed one of the fighters stood next to him. »Now we converted it into this camp. Schools are reduced in Dawla Islamya, because we teach only two subjects: The holy quoran and military training. People are encouraged to lead a simple and a devout life for Allah. The few people with expertise come from abroad.« Chris nodded and took some notes.

In the meantime word had spread that the non-believing guests by the caliph had arrived and many fighters assembled in the small room or gazed through the door. Chris went to the other corner of the room where some weapons were scattered on the floor. Kalashnikovs, explosive belts and controllers. One fighter took up a flat belt and explained: »These belts are used for self-defense. That means, especially for inexperienced or handicapped fighters. If they are caught by the enemy they can pull this trigger here« - he touched the trigger, which made Chris feel uneasy - »and they will instantly go to paradise. Chris felt relieved when he lay down the belt again. »And what are the controllers for? Can you blow something up with these as well?«, he continued to query. The men started to laugh and the Algerian answered in broken English: »With these you can only play Playstation. It's a good way to relax sometimes.«

The Syrian asked the high guests if the were hungry and Chris realized in this moment that he was actually starving. One of the fighters hurried away and returned a little later with some plastic bags. »I am sure you know, it is Ramadan right.« The Algerian looked at his watch. »But it is also time for us to eat, brothers.« They dispersed the food on the floor and sat down together. Chicken and rice with pita bread was served. For drinks they had milk and Pepsi whit the etiquette stripped off. During dinner they were told about the next steps. This night they would spend in a safe house where their luggage would be checked and they had to leave all electronic devices like phones and laptops etc. While the Algerian was speaking, Chris felt that slight unease creeping up again.

»Hi Luis, Mandy and Therese are in town. Want to join us with a bump please?« Luis saw the message on his phone and instantly felt a rush of energy. With Mandy it was always promising to be a fun night. It was midnight and he had almost fallen asleep, but he would take care of that in a minute. He pulled out a big box out of his nightstand and put it on the table. Not long ago he had bought some of the best quality cocaine from Mexico. It was called Jesu Cristo. And it was really enlightening like a touch of god. Luis was known for the best quality. He relied on his good reputation of not stretching too much. And for his premium clients he offered the best cocaine you could get in the Miami area. But he was convinced that as a drug dealer you also had some responsibility for your clients. Mandy and Therese would jump right from the rooftop if they snorted pure Jesu Cristo. So he had to stretch it just a little so they would have the perfect kick. When he was done, he drew a line for himself to perk up. He knew it was Ramadan and all, but he was glad he was on a good way to gradually reducing his consume until he finally didn't need it any longer. His new faith helped him a great deal in that journey of pursuing the right things. Before he was a real mess. He had an effervescent temper in Opa-locka and that alone was a bad combination. He knew he had caused his mother a great deal of worries in the past. He snorted the line and put some cocaine in his mouth and tongue. Soon he would be able to leave that ultimate vice behind him. But for now, it was just too good. He dressed and jumped on his motorbike. The Triumph bonville had been the mashine of his father. It was his pride. Driving through the city gave him a sense of meditation. He could let go of his negative thoughts and find bliss in his solitude. A little bit like praying for Allah. He imagined how he soon would find another job and leave all that crap behind. He needed just some more money and then he would be gone from Opa-locka. He pictured his sister's face when he would brake the news.

After a refreshing ride he finally arrived at the *Dream Hotel South Beach,* where the party was going down. the hot spot for the rich and beautiful. Luis would have not even allowed to enter the lobby if Mandy had not put him on the guest list, not to mention the *Highbar* at the rooftop. He walked around the pool which was all white and gazed at the Atlantic who was less than 30 meters below. The scenery was unreal. In a golden cage next to him two girls in a white bikini and a captain's hat were dancing to the rhythmic lounge music. Luis strolled through the bar and looked out for Mandy. He found her sitting on a white sofa chatting with her friends. She jumped up when she saw him und hugged him. »So cool that you are here, the party sucks!« She signaled her friend to come and they left for the toilets. Luis presented them Jesu Cristo and the girls chuckled in anticipation. »The best powder from here to Medellin. You will feel like you're in the metrocable to Medellin. Check this out.« The girls snorted the lines with their personalized snuff bullets and let it seep in. Mandy gave him 200 Dollars for a little bag and they stepped outside. He said goodbye to the girls and strolled to the edge of the rooftop to watch over the quiet sea. That was the reason why it was so difficult to quit. You could earn a lot of money in Miami by being a drug dealer. But unlike other drug dealers Luis didn't live a luxury life. He saved it all until he had enough money to leave it all behind. Inshallah.

Carl opened the gate to the prison courtyard and pointed at a young man, who was sitting at a bench. Adriana had arranged this meeting immediately after Ortega had gave her a contact. »Ali, you have a visitor.« The policeman made a gesture and the two other men left the bench. The young man had been captured on his way to syria with a book in his luggage called »how to kill an infidel« and other material from al quaida and was sentenced to 4 years without parole. Adriana greeted the man. »Hallo, my name is Adriana. I am a psychiatrist and I would like to reassess your eligibility for parole«, she lied. »Alright, shoot.« Ali answered halfheartedly. Adriana pulled out her pad. »You wanted to join the Islamic State. Can you tell me for what reason?« Ali looked at her condescending. »The main reason is to obey the will of Allah.« Adriana was prepared for a conversation filled with ideology. »Let's take the latest attack of the so called Black jack. What do you feel, when innocent people and children are killed in name of Allah?« Ali laughed sarcastically. »Innocent? Who is innocent? The west is fighting the muslims for decades. They killed hundreds of thousands of innocent women and children in Afghanistan, Iraq and the list goes on. And all of that is based on lies. So I can understand that some brothers might seek revenge for that injustice. An eye for an eye, and a tooth for a tooth. That's from the Bible if I'm not mistaken.« He laughed again. »But is this an official position of the Islamic State or is it just individuals who take it into their own hands?« Adriana kept asking. »Well, there is a fatwa by the Caliph where he mentions this. He said, how can a muslim sleep while his brothers are bombed and murdered by the western enemies. Fight the Kufar where you meet them with whatever weapons you have at hand. If you don't have a weapon at least spit them in their face!« His look had turned malign and it gave Adriana creeps. She glanced towards Carl who was standing some feet away. She wanted to end the conversation as fast as possible, but she had one last question. »But you personally didn't want to do an attack on american soil but rather emigrate to syria. Why?« The young man stroked his beard. »I wanted to help build the Islamic State. Like Israel is a religious State I wanted to help build a muslim state where the believers can live according to the laws of Allah. The pure Sharia, not the corrupted Sharia like in Saudi Arabia or other so called muslim countries. That is the obligation of every true muslim.« He added. In that moment the bell rang and the inmates had to return to their cells. Adriana thanked Ali for his time and Carl escorted her outside.

Chapter 7

Her mother prepared the dinner in the kitchen, wile Adriana fetched the newspaper. A moment later Adriana stood in the door with a pale face and read the headline. »The gun ban is here!« Adriana read the article. »The president has made use of his executive rights passed a temporary ban on weapon sells for private use. Gun owner are allowed to keep their guns.« She couldn't believe her eyes. »The president argues that the 2. Amendment of the constitution - the right to bear arms had to be weighed against the constitutional right of safety. The current situation with increasing attacks and massacres by radicalized young people justified the constraints on the 2. Amendment.« She put away the newspaper consternated. »Pero tesoro, that's a good thing. Finally the president has acted decisively.« Adriana nodded her head. She switched on the TV and zapped through the news channels till she stayed with a reporter: »We are in the heart of New York where a huge crowd of about 200.000 people has gathered to protest against the gun ban. Demonstrators have occupied the Wall Street and the Zucotti Park. A lot of the people brought their guns and hold them in the air in protest. Their slogan is: »We are the 90 %.« It has turned into a volatile atmosphere. By now the police limited itself on observing the situation and speaking out warnings. But it can get out of control any moment. Taylor Jennings, Can, New York.«

Adriana switched off the TV. She didn't know what to believe. She had a feeling. They argued that they wanted to stop the terror attacks by the gun ban. But in Opa-locka for example anybody could get a gun on the streets in any moment. She wondered if that was the right measure to stop the attacks from occurring.

She had to think of Zaidi. In the past few days he didn't open up a bit. She was at a dead end. Usually after 3. 4 sessions she managed to make them talk to her. Especially when they have already given a full confession of their deed. But Black Jack had shut down completely after the first meeting. After the conversation with Ali she had so many questions and she needed to brake his blockade. She thought of her best friend Bergen. They had studied psychiatry together and had often talked cases. She had taken over her father's private practice and expanded it. The clinic was known all over Florida. Her advice was precious to Adriana. She called her friend and they arranged to meet in the chic restaurant Sazon for some enchiladas. »Adriana, my dear! You look gorgeous!« They hugged intimately and sat down on the picturesque terrace. Bergen put down her Louis Vuitton bag on the chair next to her and faced Adriana. She was the stereotype *Rich Kid* and the exact opposite of Adriana. But when she had found out that the men were all going crazy for that cuban girl, she had invited her to get to know her. After a short while the cuban

41

girl turned out to be neither superficial nor vane like the rest of her friends but rather insightful and clever. She was surprised to learn that Adriana had managed to get a stipendium for Miami U. Besides she was impressed by her work ethics. While her other friends came from rich families, Adriana had worked in supermarkets and bars during her entire studies. So they inevitably became best friends. And they loved to talk about their cases. Bergen was also an excellent and creative psychiatric. She sometimes used rather unconventional methods if necessary but almost always yielded the right results. They drank their favorite Batida de coco and enjoyed the view. »You know my offer is still valid? I am looking for a partner I can trust, as my clinic is expanding.« At every meeting Bergen repeated her offer and Adriana was tempted. But right now she enjoyed the high profile cases at the court. »Be assured, we will eventually work together, but now I need your help with a case. »You heard about the Black Jack killer?« Bergen twitched and sat upright. »Oh wow, sure. That's interesting.« Adriana told her of her first encounter with Zaidi and her problems of getting him to speak. »I don't know how to crack him«, she ended her summary. »Do you have any ideas?«

Bergen fumbled with her sunglasses. »The way I understand you don't quite know if he can't tell you more or if he doesn't want to tell you more. After all he might have a partial amnesia. That happens a lot.« She lay down her glasses and folded her hands. »I remember a case where a young girl was brought to me by her mother. She suffered from panic attacks whenever she was standing at busy crossroads. Her mother was desperate because in a city like this busy crossroads are everywhere. The girl and the mother had no idea what could have been the trigger for this reaction. They really wanted to know, but as hard as they tried, they didn't know. So I tried hypnosis. Because the conscious mind is sometimes like a overprotective mother. It wants to keep you save and in order to do that it shuts things out or paints them in another color. But the subconscious is like a sponge. It saves all the information especially if connected with emotions.

So I put her in a trance state and channeled her awareness. I shut everything out so she could focus on my voice only. When the conscious was gone she didn't construe or question, she was her pure self. In this state I asked her again what happened at a busy crossroad. And she told her that her best friend had a dog. They were at a crossroad and the dog leapt in the street and was run over by a car. Everything was full of blood. She was traumatized. « Bergen took a sip of her drink. Adriana nodded. It was worth a try. She would hypnotize Black Jack.

Chapter 8

They were brought to the so called safe house by three masked grim looking fighters. »These guys do the dirty work«, Chris thought to himself. During the ride there was a music playing Chris had heard before. It was the unofficial hymn of the Islamic State. An inarbuably nice melody, almost like meditation music. »What does the arabic refrain say?« Chris wanted to know. The fighter in the passenger seat turned around and shot back in broken English.«It says, Dawla erected from the Jihad of the pious!« Chris took a note. »I thought music is not allowed according to the interpretation of the Caliph?« The bulky guy turned around again. »That is true. Music arouses and eventually leads to adultery. But this is a gnashed. It is a song for Allah. That is allowed of course.« He turned up the volume. Chris felt like in a gangster movie, as they dashed over the bumpy road in the moonlit night and the Kalshnikows jumped in the rhythm of the street.

The entrance to the safe house was almost invisible from the street, as it was covered with thick coppice. They drove through the woods until they reached a small house. Chris felt queasy with the thought of spending the night with these three gentlemen in a place like this. They are led into a small room which was heated by a diesel-generator. One of the men took of his mask, the bulky guy kept his mask on. The third one took a stand outside of the house. The young man who showed his face told them his name was Mohamad. »Of course that is not my real name, but for you it's Mohamad«, he added with his French accent. Paulsen and Chris were summoned to hand over their electronic devices like smartphones and laptops. »Don't worry,« the French said. »It's for your own security. We don't want the enemy to locate and drop bombs on us... do we?«

He took the phones and laptops and meticulously started searching the baggage for hidden devices. Every toothpaste and every box was scrutinized. After they hadn't found anything incriminating, the tension immediately decreased and the tone became more friendly. The French ordered the bulky one to bring tea, Cola and nuts and they engaged in a lively conversation. »You remind me of my room mate in Paris.« The French told Chris. »I was studying Electrical Engineering back then. We lead a life of sex, drugs and rock'n'roll, you know what I mean?« Chris was dumbfounded by the drastic change from frighteningly scary to super nice. »Really? I studied Electrical Engineering for 1 semester, but I quit.« They laughed. »But then I came to a point in my life where I was sick with all of that. There had to be a higher meaning to life.« Chris nodded pensively. »So I began to study the holy book and found out that this was the right path towards happiness for me. I left the bad influences behind and sought to have like minded friends that looked to be good muslims. When I learnt that there is a place where a muslim can live without discrimination I had to join the movement and help build Dawla Islamic!« He looked at him with misty eyes. »Every fighter with a family is given an own house! I live with my two children and a wife in my own house now. And you get a decent salary, a part of which goes to the poor and sick people. So we have no homeless people here.« He added proudly. Paulsen grew more and more uneasy, because he knew what was going on. It was the beginning of a typical brainwash and he was concerned for Chris who apperently didn't know he was being targeted. »Yeah, that sounds like you achieved your personal goals. »Chris congratulated him. Paulsen had to step in. He cleared his throat. »But as a reasonable person, do you think it is just to butcher people with a different believe? And have slavery? Or to apply the 1500 year old Quoran to our modern times literally?« The French smiled condescendingly. »No my friend, you don't understand what you are talking about. You are retorting the propaganda of the enemy. I suppose you do it involuntary because you don't know better. First of all, we don't kill the infidels right away. If we conquer an area the adherer of the book religions, that is the Jews and Christians, have the opportunity of paying the Dschizya, which is a small tax. If they chose to do so, they can live without discrimination and even will be protected by the Islamic State.« He looked at Chris for approval. »And the issue with the slavery is also twisted. I can tell you that the life according to the rules of Allah here is just and beautiful.«

Paulsen wanted to end the conversation and told them they were tired and would like to go to sleep. The fighters complied and took to their own room. When they were on their own Paulsen signaled Chris to come closer. »They might have bugs in here, so we have to be careful what we say«, he whispered. »Did you realize how he was trying to get to you?« Chris nodded his head. »Yes, don't worry. I played ingenuous in order to make him talk. That's what we journalists do. The more they think they can get to you, the more they relinquish.« Paulsen was relieved and surprised at the same time. »Ok, you got me there.« Chris laughed. »The next time, let me do my thing. I am good at these things.« Paulsen shrugged his shoulders. They prepared their sleeping bags and tried to get some sleep after an eventful day. Although the generator was running, it was cold and Chris was shaking. But he now realized how exhausted he was and it didn't take long until he fell in a deep sleep.

Zaidi was in his solitary cell which was 3x5 meter big and contained a bed and a toilet. Except for his psychiatrist he hadn't talked to a person other than the guards for 1 week. Zaidi was in a deep slumber until a noise woke him. A man with a white doctor's overall entered the room. » It's time for your medicine again, Mr. Zaidi.« His tone was casual like he

47

was talking to a child with a flu. He stood over Zaidi's bed and prepared the syringe. »No Sir, please.« Zaidi moaned. »It makes me very - clouded. I feel much better without it. Please.« The doctor shook his head while he loaded the syringe. »I explained it to you several times. You killed innocent people. After we brought you were in a very bad condition. The medicine helps you remember what happened that day so we can have a fair trial. That is what you want too, right?« Without waiting for a response he rolled up the sleeves and tied the arm. »You will perform well. And the medicine will help you focus. I promise.« He found a big vein and pushed the fluid into his body. In an instand Zaidi became dizzy and cloudy again.

Adriana watched the preliminaries of Zaidi's trial from the stance. The jury was instructed and prosecutor and attorneys filed motions. But Adriana was more interested with Zaidi. He displayed the same behavior as at their first meeting: Distracted, without orientation and confused. His eyes were directed at the first row where his parents were seated. They were obviously devastated and tried to build eye contact with their son. He looked at them but didn't seem to recognize them. After the sitting was ended Adriana approached Zaidis parents. »Mr. Zaidi, Mrs. Zaidi, I am Adriana Borrero, the psychiatric of the court.« She adressed Mrs. Zaidi because the father seemed to be absent-minded and had tears in his eyes. »I would like to talk to you in private.

Is it possible to meet somewhere?« Mrs Zaidi changed a look with her husband. »You saw that your son is in bad condition. I try to find out how to help him.« Mrs. Zaidi nodded her head. »Yes we should meet. Can you come to our house? She gave Adriana her card and thy made an appointment for the next afternoon.

Sheikh al-Walid enjoyed the view from the platform of the 124. Floor of the Burj Khalifa. From the 828 meter tall Tower he had an overview over all Dubai til the horizon. He could discern the street net, the trees, sites of water, smaller skyscrapers and houses. The architecture fan was enticed by vertical city. Suddenly a man appeared next to him and glanced down. »Asalaamalaikum, my brother.« The sheikh said without facing him. »How is the fight advancing?« The man next to him was sturdy and had a thick beard and old fashioned glasses. »Since the union of al-Nusra and Dawla Islamiya we have regained some ground. But the enemies are advancing from all sides. The Kurds supported by the west are the strongest enemy force causing a lot of damage. The sheik nodded his head. »Fortunately with money you can by men and arms.« He observed the sun set behind the horizon like a ball hit the blue net. »You will receive a new delivery of three humvees in the coming days. Where should the delivery take place?« His brother looked around and scanned the platform before he answered. »Come to the border crossing at Hafar al Batin. In 3 days.« The sheikh smiled. »It is an honor to help the cause. May Allah protect you, Nasrallah.« Without watching he headed for the elevator to watch the sunset again from the floor below.

Paulsen and Chris were served a typical Syrian breakfast consisting of eggs, bread and marmalade before they were going to ar-Raqqa. The only stopover until Mosul where the German was held prisoner. Abu Masala had come personally to pick escort the guests. He was a medium height but heavily overweight individual. His driver was masked with a scarf so that Chris could only see his dark eyes in the rearview mirror. The ride to Ar-Raqqua took about 4 hours. It was regarded as the capital of the Islamic State. When entering the city everywhere hang black flags with the shahada in arabic letters: »There is only one god.«
It was a spooky atmosphere as they rode through the heavily bombed. The drones had obviously left their marks. And no people could be seen on the streets, like in a ghost town. »The last few days several bombs were dropped on the city. That's why people prefer to stay inside.« Abu Masala breathed heavily as he sat in front of the car. The sun had warmed up the car and beads of sweat were running down his forehead. He was about the height of Chris but a heavyweight of about 130 kg. The 4 hour ride was a challenge to

him. But also Chris was relieved when they finally reached their destination. For security reasons they had chosen an apartment in the city center, amongst a lot of citizens. The apartment had four rooms and from the furniture you could see that it once was home to a family with children. Chris didn't want to imagine what had happened to that family. In any case it was now their accommodation.

The group had assembled in the living room that was lit with candles. They took a rest from the ride with tea and some nuts. Abu Masala took a handful of nuts and explained with a smile. »We are travelers that is why are allowed have an exception from the rules of Ramadan.«

Chris was amazed about the fact that they had an explanation for everything. Even the most dreadful inhumane practices. »Can you explain a thing to me«, he began. »Christians and Jews have the choice to pay a tax that protects them. Why don't have shiites the same rights? They are muslims after all« Abu Masala shook his head vehemently. »They have to convert to the real Islam or they are killed! You know, they were the enemies of the prophet Mohameed, praised be his name. So there was no lenience towards them.« He clarified. Chris wanted to test his rhetorics. »I understand. But then also other Sunni groups who have the almost identical doctrine of a caliphate are enemies to the islamic State.« Abu Masala grew impatient and annoyed with the questioning. »There is only one caliphate and that is

Dawla Islamiya. Everyone who denies that is regarded an enemy and will be killed!«

In the evening another young man called Abu Lot joined them. » You might know the story from the old testament when Lot fought the homosexuals«, the young man stated without digression. »In those times there were fornication and demoralisation. Sodom and gomorra. In the same extent that we have in our time.« Abu Masala nodded his head frantically and encouraged his friend to go on. »Everybody drinks and fornicates and the vilest man receives the highest respect.« He looked at Chris who nodded. »And that's the reason I chose this name, because like Lot I fight against Sodom and Gomorra.« With that punchline he finished his impressive introduction. Chris had to bite his tongue to not start laughing out loud. The young man reminded him of Mohamed Ali in his prime. But as funny as it seemed, it was serious business. And the whole topic around the lack of restraint in the western societies seemed to be a major argument in the indoctrination of these young men.

Suddenly there was a big bang and turmoil the streets, as if a raid had begun. The four men jumped out on the balcony to see what was going on. Abu Masala took his phone to call somebody. After a few moments he exclaimed. »These are celebration shots. We have conquered a new city in Iraq!« Abu Lot joined in the cheering. The night sky of Raqqa looked like at a new year's eve, only less colorful. But Abu Lot's eyes glistened and he wanted to celebrate with his brothers on the streets. Chris asked if he could join him and Abu Masala didn't have any objections. Abu Lot took his Kalashnikov to add to the firework and they sped off.

The very streets that were empty in the afternoon were now packed with people. On the main street there was a big screen where the news of the latest conquest were broken. They joined the crowd. And Abu Lot greeted his friends. Chris didn't understand the words but the video was clearly propaganda material. Filled with dramatic cuts and slow motion effects almost like in the Matrix. But for the almost exclusively young men it was all cheers and hugs. While Abu Lot was distracted with his friends, Chris seized the opportunity to talk to another nordic looking fighter who turned out to be Swedish. Chris was surprised. »I thought Sweden was the country with the best educational system and the lowest crime rates and the best standard of living...« He looked puzzled at the blond man with his reddish beard. »Yes it's true. Sweden is a safe and nice place. I work here and return once a year to my family. But look at this. This is amazing, isn't it.« Chris nodded exuberantly and left the man. He was either a mercenary or psychopath. Or both. Abu Lot found Chris and told him to return to the apartment.

Chapter 9

Adriana was heading out to West Miami to meet the Zaidis.
It was one of the noble suburbs of Miami. The gate opened
automatically and the drove up to the house. She had learnt
from the file that Mr. Zaidi had made it to riches with his
import-export company. And the mansion was quite impressive. »Hallo Mrs. Zaidi.« She greeted the woman who received her at the door. »Oh please call me Sara.« She gave Adriana a warm handshake and led her inside. She felt that
Sara was eager to talk to someone. She skipped the courte-
sies and asked Adriana right away. »What did they do with
my son? And why is his own mother not allowed to visit?
This is not normal, is it?« Her voice trembled and was rau-
cous from crying. Adriana tried to be objective. »I had a view
encounters and he seems to suffer from enormous stress.«
She watched Sara closely. »Do you know anything about a
drug addiction in the past?« Sara snuffled indignantly. »My
son never consumed drugs. Not even when his friends were
smoking a joint. He was a little nerd, if you will. All he was
interested in was science and music.« She was about to cry.
Adriana felt compassion for her. It was a terrible thing for
every mother, if her son became a murderer. Let alone a
mass murderer. And the reactions were the same: Negation,
repression and self accusation. Sara seemed to be in the first
phase. »Sara, how are you and your husband holding up

with all of this?« She asked emphatically. Sara sighed. »It's a tough situation for us. And it's so - unbelievable. Like a nightmare. And every morning you wake up you hope that it was just nightmare and your son is well and out there doing what he likes to do. But then reality kicks in and - it's the worst. Like I don't want to live anymore. My life is over if he really did what they say.« She paused and kept fighting against the tears. »But what really upsets me is the way the prosecutor, the police and the media are handling this case. As if the story was already written. A psychopathic islamist ran amok. Full stop. No question asked. Is that a fair trial? That makes me sad.« She wearily took a sip of tea. »But he wasn't that person. Everybody who knew him could tell you that right away. He was the best student in his senior year. He was a nerd. But he was not a loner. He couldn't give more of a damn about religion. HE WASN'T THAT PER-SON!« She repeated exasperatedly. Adriana had listend closely and took some notes. »Can you tell me about your husband?« »My husband is Tunesian and Muslim. At the age of 20 years he came here to enjoy the freedoms and liberties of the west. He was never a religious person. And he never spoke with Yusuf about religion.« Adriana scribbled something on her pad. »What did Yusuf study again?« »My son studied near sciences. And after his bachelor he specialized in the science of the mind at the university of Colorado. He was fascinated with all the things revolving around mind altering and mind control. He was so excited when he told us about it. He moved to Colorado last year and in the beginning he was so enthusiastic about it. He loved the Campus, the new friends. Everything but the weather. We spoke every 3 days or at least on the weekends. But the last semester he somewhat got more distant. I don't know if it had to do with that program he joined or if he had a girlfriend. Fact is, he always told us he had to work. We were looking forward for the Christmas holidays to see him again. But then we saw him on TV - as a convict. « Sara's broke into tears and Adriana padded her shoulder. »I can't believe this is happening to me.« Adriana waited until Sara had regained her composure. She wanted to know one last thing. » Sara, the police said, they found more weapons and explosives in your son's apartment. Do you believe, your son was able to build an explosive device?« Sara laughed a bitter laugh. » Like I said, the last semester we didn't have so much contact. But before he couldn't even fix a puncture on his bike. Let alone an explosive device. And what for? It doesn't make sense.« Adriana took some notes. The more she learnt about the case she became more puzzled. She wanted to say goodbye, when Sara gave her a pice of paper. »Please contact this young man. He was a witness at the shooting. He will be able to answer some more questions.« Adriana took the piece of paper and left with a friable feeling in her stomach.

Chapter 10

Chubbs got stitch. He ran as fast as he could with his shopping cart that contained all of his belongings. He hoped that he made it in time for a bed in the barracks. For months he had been sleeping there. There were beds and tables and couches protected by the rain by provisional walls and roofs. Almost like a real home for the homeless. And there were always more contenders for the few places. The last real estate crisis had washed up even more people on the streets. With more than 40.000 homeless, Miami was on top of all American cities. The situation was so drastic that private initiatives were founded to help the poorest. The barracks were pulled up illegally in a cloak and dagger operation on an empty space in the midst of Miami. They had expanded so it increasingly became a thorn in the side of the authorities. Chubbs was there since the first days. But as the word had spread the fight for the desired few beds was grew harder. Today Chubbs was late and that was why he paced. The alternative was sleeping on the streets and that was a threat for his well-being and his few belongings. He arrived panting and waved at Max, the founder of the barracks. He was known to be strict and refuse anybody if the barracks were full. No matter who he was. »Hey Chubbs, I'm afraid you are late tonight.« He told him right away. Chubbs didn't want to believe it. »Max, I had to deal with important things. I really need shelter for tonight. For as long as we know each other.« Max shook his head. »I understand, but if there is no vacant place I can't do anything for you. You know how to is, first come first serve.« Chubbs turned around and cursed. He had to find another place to sleep. But he had one ace up its sleeve. A place in the canalization of Miami. It wasn't as comfortable as the barracks but still better than the streets. The run-outs of the canalization were usually dry. Only with heavy rain the water level in the pipes rose. The downside was that it took one hour by. And he hated to go by train. Even the poor people watched him in disgust as if he were an animal. But he had no other option.

When he finally reached the canalization he carefully turned around and watched. He didn't want people to know of his place. Because he didn't want to lose it. When he saw nobody around he sneaked through the entrance. The pipe was 8 feet high and pitch black. His only source of light were some matches. But he knew the way by heart. He slowly walked through the ankle deep waste water and turned into a smaller pipe after 200 meters. In the pipe he had to crouch down and after 20 meters he reached his spot. He lighted a match and was relieved to find everything like he had left it the last time. The floor was dry and covered with newspapers, cartons and garbage. In the beginning he had lived here with his former wife. But then she couldn't take it no more. She had found some other man and moved in with him. And he was still here. He pulled out his bottle of rum that he had bought and took a big numbing sip. What else to do if past, present and future were painful. He embraced the numbness in his mind and shortly after he fell asleep.

Chris and Paulsen were ready for the stage to Mosul. But Abu Masala had bad news for them. »Our driver had an accident yesterday and the fender is damaged. We have to repair it before we can go to Mosul. Today is Friday prayer and people work only until prayer time we will not be able to make it today.« Chris sighed disappointedly. »But you can accompany us to the mosque if you like.« Abu Lot offered with a smile. Chris was relieved. No journalist before has seen a prayer of the Islamists in Raqqa. They were accompanied by Abu Lot, Abu Masala, the driver with the lazy eyes and another masked fighter. The group strolled to the nearby market, which was bustling with people like the one in Gaziantep. The only difference was that the people were dressed less colorful than in the Turkish city. Black dominated the streets. There were almost no women on the streets and the few that did go out were dressed in a niqab. Chris wanted to have one of these harem pants that most of the fighters were wearing in order to blend in with the rest. They stepped into a shop and found one in Chris's size. It was a nice shade of black, Chris was thinking to himself. When he wanted to pay, Abu lot held him back. »You are guests by the Caliph, you don't have to pay!« Chris changed a look with the vendor who affirmed that and added that he was honored to be able to give him a present. He was clearly under pressure but Chris couldn't undermine the authority of Abu Lot. So he had no other choice than thanking the man and wishing him the best. It was almost 12 a.m. and people were closing shops and hurrying towards the mosque. Although there were dark clouds hovering in the sky and it had begun to rain and the loamy soil was wet and slippery. When they turned around the corner they saw the mighty mosque. It was a surreal sight. The mosque was apparently so packed that people were gathering in front of the mosque. People put their jackets or cartons on the muddy ground in order to pray. He couldn't help but noticing that most of the crowd were young men and probably foreign fighters as well. Chris and Paulsen took seats in a restaurant that was open to old and handicapped people attending the prayer. Chris got a freshly pressed passion fruit juice and some nuts and watched the prayer to begin. The voice of the Imam started blaring through the speakers shouting Allahu'akbar joined by the crowd. It send cold shivers down Chris' spine. The Imam kept talking and although Chris didn't understand a word he felt that they were no words of peace and charity. Paulsen looked over his shoulder and saw that the 2 guards were standing out of hearing distance. « The Imam is saying, the west is trying to destroy their paradise on earth. But the non-believers will pay the price for such behavior. Our path led by Allah the almighty is the only right path under guidance of the Quoran. Let's march in, oh soldiers of Allah!« The crowd joined in his shouting ,Allahu'akbar. Chris watched at Paulsen in disbelief: »You speak arabic and kept it a secret the whole time? Now you got me surprised.« Paulsen smiled but put a finger to his lips. »Hushhh. You never know, it might be an advantage one time.« After the prayer was over, the guards turned their attention to the Germans. »Did you like it?« Abu Lot slapped Chris on the shoulder and laughed. He was in a good mood like always. »Yes deeply moving, I especially liked the happy end.« Chris joked back and they laughed. He had a strange connection to Abu Lot who was an interesting yet disturbing character. »The show is over! Let's go home.« Lazy Eyes yelled. Chris noted that the crowd was swaying in different direction as if they were heading somewhere. »Where are the people going?« Chris asked curiously. »Everybody goes home, and we do the same!« Lazy Eyes shouted angrily. Chris had the feeling that he was not telling the truth. The crowd was rather preparing for something. And Chris was curious as to what it was. He bend down to his knees to tie his shoelaces. When his guards didn't pay attention he slipped away and submerged in the crowd. People were headed in the direction of a square where a stage was erected. Chris rushed to front in order to have good view. Suddenly he felt a firm grip on his arm. »Hey you, here you are!« Chris was and slowly appalled tuned around. To his surprise he recognised the Swedish man from the day before. Chris gave him a relieved smile.

»That was a good prayer. What is going on here?« The Swedish laughed. »Yeah the prayer was nice, but this is even better. Some sinners are punished for their deeds.« He pointed at the stage.« It's about to begin.« Chris turned his attention to the stage where now 8 black clad fighters were standing in the backround. In the front appeared a moderator uttered some introductory words. The Swedish translated for Chris. » This man sold alcohol in his shop despite having been warned twice. Now according to the Sharia he gets 30 whip lashes.« The crown erupted in cheers and shouted »AllahuAkbar!« The executioner nodded with his head and the trembling man subserviently uncovered his back. He made him bend on his knees and took the lash. »Paaatsch!« The sound of the hard leather on the soft flesh was ear-pearcing until the last rows. »Paaatsch!« Every whip was accompanied by a fanatic »Allahu'Akbar« by the crowd. Chris had goose bumps. After the 15. Whip he had to turn his gaze away. The back of the man was all blood and flesh and he was in such shock that he couldn't even scream any more. When the torture was over, he was carried away under the roar of the crowd. The executioner reappeared with a veiled woman and her father. »This woman is an adulterer. She had put shame on her family and you know what is the punishment for adultery according to the Sharia!« The crowd answered unisono: »Stoning!« The executioner nodded his head satisfiedly and turned to the woman: The punishment is the consequence of your deeds. No one had coerced you in doing what you did. That is why you have to accept the verdict of Allah.« He stood in front of her and glazed at her. »Do you accept the the verdict of Allah?« The woman looked intimidatedly to her father. »Please forgive me father. I didn't want to put shame on you.« Her father spat on the ground. »No I can't, I have no daughter. Any longer.« The woman cried and slightly nodded to the exeecutioner. »I accept the verdict.« The executioner turned to her father. »Do you want to say something to your daughter before she will get her punishment?« His voice trembled. »I recommend to every woman that she protects her honor more than her life!« The executioner tied the legs of the girl and led her to a pit next to the stage. Only her upper body stuck out of the surface. People stepped closer and reached for the stones that lay around. The father took the first stone and fired it at his daughter. As soon as he was done the crowd joined in and threw stones at the poor creature who was screaming and shouting. The crowd was thirsty for blood. He saw the Swedish throw a big stone at her head. The girl was barely moving any more.

Chris couldn't bear the sight and blazed his trail through the brawling crowd.

He rushed back to the apartment where Lazy Eyes was waiting for him impatiently in the streets. »You sneaked away intentionally! You were not allowed to see that?« He yelled at Chris with sparkling eyes. »No, I didn't sneak away. I tied my laces and when I looked up, everybody was gone.« Chris tried to explain himself. »You infidel liar!« Lazy Eyes was furious now. He picked his gun from his holster and pointed it at Chris. Suddenly Paulsen stood in between them and looked Lazy Eyes right in his eyes. »Whatever you think he did, we are still guests by the Caliph Abu Bakr al Bagdadi! Our safety was guaranteed by him and if you pull the trigger now, you will be the next one to be punished.« Zaidi hesitated with his hand on the trigger. In the meantime Abu Lot had appeared. »He is right, put the gun away.« They changed an intense look. »PUT the gun away!« Lazy Eyes sighed and stomped away. It took some minutes until Chris heart rate was down to normal again. When they had a moment to themselves Paulsen whispered. »He probably is not only driver but from the secret service. Watch out.«

Chapter 11

»Mr. Zaidi, please have a seat.« Adriana had arranged for him not to wear the straitjacket and prepared biscuits and a glass of milk to make him feel comfortbable. He appeared a little less confused than at the preliminaries. »How do you feel today?« »I feel better according to the circumstances.« He replied briefly. »Alright, I can see that you still don't sleep well and that the situation means a great burden to you. And I promised your Mother Sara that I wouldn't push your boundaries now. Because I am not only here for an expert opinion, but I am also a doctor, who cares for her patients. Now, before we continue with the screening I want you to try this exercise in order to ease the tension. Do you agree to that?« Zaidi took another biscuit and nodded his head. »Yes sure, we can try.« »Good, now have another sip of milk and if you feel ready you can give me a sign with your head.« He did as suggested and nodded. »Now, as the tension in your body is captured you might feel heavy and exhausted. You might want to release the tension as your eyes are closing. Maybe you picture yourself as a stone that is sinking into deep water, sinking towards the ground. Now, the deeper and deeper you sink the less noise comes to your ears you focus on the soothing voice that you hear right now in this moment. Now the deeper you sink like a diver the sunrays are becoming less distracting you less and you might begin to see your inner light shine again. The more to let go of your resistance the deeper you can let yourself fall in that comfortable warm water. And the more you breath deeply into your lungs the more you start to relax. With every breath you take you can relax even more. And you feel safe and secure the deeper you sink into that beautiful state of bliss. And you can give me a sign if you want to leave your stress behind completely and go even deeper with me.« Yusuf nodded his head slowly. »Now, as you go deeper with every breath, you come closer to the bottom of the ground. And you might notice a chest that is illuminated by light. As you might have a feeling that there is a treasure in that box you try getting closer. Maybe it's your old self, the young Yusuf who liked to study and listen to music. Maybe you meet the Yusuf who loved to hang out with his friends and was proud of his parents. Remember when you had a good time with your parents. Imagine the laughter of your Dad.« Zaidi smiled in deep trance. Now, you also might remember the time in Colorado. Everything was so exciting for you. Maybe you had a best friend there?« Yusuf nodded. »Do you remember his name? Tell me his name!« - »Jake Riley.« »Picture yourself having a good time with Jake. Now, imagine with how much anticipation your mother expected you from Colorado. How deeply she loves you.« A single tear made its way down his cheek. »Would they understand why you killed those people?« Yusuf slowly shook his head. And if you told Jake about it, Would he understand?« Yusuf shook his head

66

again. »What would you tell your mother now, did you kill for Allah?« Yusuf hesitated but then shook his head again. »Did somebody help you in that Cinema. Suddenly the door flew open and two policemen stormed into the room and grabbed Yusuf. He looked haggardly at them, like someone who is awoken out of deep sleep. »Sorry to interrupt, but the session is over.« Adriana was perplexed and looked at Carl and Sam who had appeared in the door. »We have order to move Mr. Zaidi to another prison for security reasons. You can read that all in this note.« He passed her a note and they dragged Yusuf towards the door. Before he disappeared he turned his head to Adriana. He changed a look with Adriana and he nodded his his head slightly.

The car was repaired and they could finally go to Mosul. They were two pick-ups but because of the drones they always had to have a gap between them. Lazy Eyes was driving the car, next to him sat Abu Masala. The atmosphere was tense after the argument the day before, so Chris was relieved he sat next to Abu Lot who was chewing on a wooden stick.. »What are you chewing there?« Chris asked. Abu Lot laughed in his nonchalant manner. »That is a Siwak, it's a kind of arabic toothbrush, if you will.« He produced another stick from his bag and gave it to Chris. »Try this.« Chris pretended to bite it like an apple. »Not like this!« Both of them laughed. Abu Lot cut out a little ring at the end and showed him the technique. Chris imitated him and wrinkled his nose instantly. »That is so bitter:« Abu lot shrugged his shoulder. »I told you, you have to get used to it. We don't have electric toothbrushes here. And after a while it's fine.« Chris kept the Siwak in his mouth practicing.

The barren landscape rushed by to the melody of a nasheed. Syria existed of two thirds of clay desert. »Is it true that the Islamic State finances the war predominantly out of the revenues from the oil business?« Paulsen wanted to know, while they were passing some oil fields. »Yes that is correct. The enemy has destroyed many oil fields but the majority of oil fields are still intact. Every day we earn about 1 million dollars from the oil business.« He boasted cocky. »And as you probably know, we have our own currency. Gold, silver and bronze. That makes u independent from the international currency crises. Because you can't produce gold like currency. Which is the reason for inflation.« He had made his homework this time. He pulled a gold coin out of his pocket and displayed it. »This is 21 karat Gold. That little thing Is. worth 700 dollar. The coin weighted surprisingly much. »How many of these do you need to buy a slave?« Abu Masala pondered for a second. »A good woman costs about 3000 dollar.« Abu Lot giggled as Chris went on. »Do you have a slave?« Abu Masala started sweating. »No, I didn't have the money for that until now.« He answered contritely. »But maybe I buy one in Mossul. He rubbed his greasy hands.

»There is a story among the fighters.« Abu Lot joined in. »One brother had bought a slave for quite some money. He even made her teeth white got her hair done, invested in clothes and so on. And you know what happened?« He made a pause. »She ran away!« Abu Masala and the driver were laughing the loudest. Chris changed a irritated look with Paulsen. After a while of listening to the nasheed the driver turned the music down. »Do you know what this place is?« Outside were some policemen of the Islamic State and some black flags. It looked like a normal checkpoint. »This is the former Sykes-Pikot line that separated Syria from Iraq. But we erased that from the map. Dawla Islamic has no borders, we will conquer the world.« His brothers cheered him on in his rant and they waved their brothers outside.

It had begun to rain and Lazy Eyes rode at a good pace on the wet road. On both lanes there was some busy traffic and especially the lorries slowed down the traffic. As the other lane was full and a lorry was in front of them, Lazy Eyes accelerated to overhaul him on the right, where the emergency lane usually is. But here it was just a muddy area. As he touched the glassy surface, the car didn't react anymore and faded into the the muddy area. He stopped the car and reignited it again. When he tried to drive slowly the cars spinned skidding mud in all directions but the car was stuck. »Well done!«, Abu Masala applauded ironically. »Everybody out of the car. We need to push it out of the mud.« He ordered. »You too! I take over the wheel.« They counted from three

69

to one and pushed as hard as they could while Abu Masala pushed the gas down. The car fishtailed but didn't make it out of the mud. They tried another and another time until Abu Lot took over the wheel. After only one try he made it out of the pit. Chris and Lazy Eyes kept hanging on as the car gained speed, sliding on the muddy ground like ice princesses. It was like a challenge between the two. ‚Who let go first loses‘. The car accelerated more in order to gain enough momentum to make it up the slope to the street again. They eyed each other but neither of them let go. Suddenly Abu Masala yerked the steering wheel to the left and sped up the slope and made it to the street. He stopped the car and got out. They exclaimed in joy and gave high fives. However, when they looked for Lazy Eyes he was not to be found. They watched down the slope and saw him lying in the mud. At first they laughed but when they came closer they noticed the pain in the face of Lazy Eyes. »I think my leg is broken.« He moaned. Abi Masala and Paulsen had caught up with them and they hauled the injured into the car. »We have to get him to the hospital right away.« Paulsen suggested. Fortunately the were close to Mosul and it didn't take long to reach the hospital. They got out and within minutes they ordered a doctor to take care of their brother. They accompanied him to the emergency room and stayed outside. Chris excused himself to go to the bathroom. When he had washed the mud out of his face he made a detour before returning to the group. He had seen a hall with injured Islamic State fighters, with black flags on the walls. He entered the room where about 40 injured men lay. It was a shocking sight. Lacerated extremities, Shot wounds and blood everywhere. He approached one fighter who looked European. »Are you going back to battle?« He asked him rhetorically. The poor man with only one leg managed to put a smile on his face. »Yes not only to battle, I will go to paradise soon.« He answered belligerently and put up the ,One God' sign.

Sheikh al-Walid reached the Kingdom Center, The necklace of Riad as the called it for its parabolic arch. When he entered the conference room of the hotel, everybody was already sitting at the big mahagoni table. He saw Miller, Jed Collins and Nasrallah and 5 other men. »Asalaamalaikum, gentlemen«, he greeted the illustrious group. He sat down and Jed Collins took over. »How benign of you, sheikh, that we can finally begin.« He reprimanded him. »We have assembled to assess the situation. The United States has a vital interest in peace in the region. I don't need to explain the importance of Syria and Iraq. We are supporting the opposition to Assad where ever we can in order to promote human rights and democracy. But in the recent past some of the groups we support and that are here assembled - he looked around - seemed to follow their own agenda, causing major attacks in the west, and especially in the US. It should be clear that this has to end as of now.« He slapped his fist on the table. »The next time an attack takes place on American soil with any - I repeat any jihadist involvement - funding and logistic support of all here assembled will be suspended immediately. Is that clear to everybody?« There was an uproar but Jed Collins was not finished. »I don't care what you tell your followers, but I'm sure you will be creative.« He paused for a moment. »Do you have any questions? No? Good, because it's really simple. You are dismissed.« The group slowly made its way to the door. Only Nasrallah remained seated.

Jed Collins poured two glasses of whiskey and they clinked glasses. »It's been a long time. And we have achieved a lot.« The CIA man congratulated his friend. »But the Syrian regime is still in power and with the support of the Russians we are in the cold war again. Nasrallah agreed. »And we are the pawns in the game. We know that.« He took another sip. »What game are you playing, Jed? You really want to quit funding us? You know what happens. The Kurds come flying at us. Within one month all opposition groups will be eradicated.« Jed Collins nodded. »We just don't want any more attacks on American soil, that's all.« The Iraqi looked inquisitive at Jed Collins. »You Americans don't have loyalty.« Jed Collins got angry. »Hey, who is sending you money to buy weapons, who is sending you tanks, who is sending you fighters willing to die for Allah. And all you do is complaining about loyalty. Are you serious? I tell you something. There are influential people who have serious doubts that it is worth one cent spending in you guys. I keep telling them they should be patient and the momentum has shifted bla bla. I fight for you! And you have the guts to tell me about loyalty?« Nasrallah took another sip. »You are right, I'm sorry. Good to hear that you still believe in us. I hope we can make advances again.« They shook hands and were about to leave. »One last thing«, Nasrallah asked, »the gun ban in the US, has that anything to do with us?« Jed Miller shook his head. »Not that I know of. The president wanted to take a measure of restoring the peace. These attacks got really out of hand. We want this to stop.«

»What a mess. If I had known this, I would have put on rubber boots«, the taller of the two men are grumbling, when they stepped through the canalisation. They had a big flashlight and a heat camera with them. »There on the right.« The smaller man indicated. They ducked down and stepped through the smaller pipe where Chubbs was sleeping. »Here we go.« The taller guy blinded Chubbs with the flashlights. He woke up and stared into the lights bedazzled. Before he could say anything, the taller man punched him in the face and knocked him out.
They carried him out and lifted him in the trunk of the car.

Chapter 12

Sitting in the Metrorail Adriana called Ortega. She needed to speak to someone. »Something is quite odd in this case. I get more and more doubts that Yusuf does not fit the profile of a terrorist.« She told him about their session and the sudden interruption by the FBI. »They took them right under my nose, shortly before I was about to get him to talk.« Adriana calmed down. »Something is odd. Maybe you can find out what this is all about?« Ortega was not keen on snooping around without permission. »You said, he had confessed. Don't you think that's enough?« »Come to my place tomorrow and we talk it over. Maybe you are right and I worked myself up about this matter.

Abu Masala informed Paulsen and Chris that they were to meet the person in charge of the prisoner Koletzki the next day. Paulsen was relieved. »That is good news!« Abu Masala nodded his head respectfully. »As we have nothing to do today, I would like suggest to visit the site of the battle for Mosul outside the gates.« Paulsen added. Chris was surprised hearing a sightseeing proposal from Paulsen, but it was a good idea. »I think, that's possible.« Abu Masala replied. After breakfast they took to their cars and rode to the main gate of Mosul where according to the narrative 183 Jihadists had defeated the iraqi army of 40.000 men. They passed the gate that were guarded by Islamic state fighters and rode onto the adjacent battle field. They got out of the car and glanced at the field which was about the size of 20 football pitches. They had left everything untouched, so there were dozens of rusty tanks, military vehicles and guns in all shapes. »That is quite a playground.« Abu Lot laughed and padded on Chris' shoulder who shook his head in disbelief. He climbed on a tank overlooking the battle field. »At first we orchestrated suicide attacks at strategic points. That caused panic among the enemy lines. »Abu Masala recounted. »We then moved up with the 2nd row and caused more havoc. Bullets were flying everywhere but Allah protected his fighters.«

Paulsen was sick of the propaganda stories and joined Chris. »On this place thousands of young men died. Ripped to pieces, burnt to death or simply shot«, he ruminated. Chris nodded his head. He pictured the brainwashed fighters racing towards paradise.

»We have to get to the cars fast.« Abu Masala interrupted their contemplation. »There is a drone in the sky. We are too conspicuous with our two pick-ups.« Chris looked up into the sky and discovered the shiny object. Hastily they hurried back to the apartment but the shiny bird was still up in the sky trailing them. Abu Masala became more and more nervous. Suddenly everyone was gone and Paulsen and Chris found themselves left alone in the apartment. »We shoudln't stay inside.« Paulsen suggested. Chris had noted a nearby

75

football pitch where some young men had been playing. Even now they didn't bother the drone hovering over their heads. Chris joined them playing while the drone was circling in the sky. The game was fast and he started sweating. He rolled up his pants and only now realized that he looked like a Jihadist. Whereas those people where clearly civilians. After the game was over the player shook hands and gathered on the side. Some of them smoked a cigarette, which was not permitted under Sharia law. But they apparently had nothing to fear. Chris wanted to talk to them. It was the first opportunity to talk to civilians without his entourage. He asked the young man who gave him three assists for a cigarette. »You smoke? Are you not a fighter of Dawla Islamiya?« He asked surprised. »No, I am not a fighter. Me and my friend are invited by the jihadists«, he didn't want to go into the details, »to conduct some business.« »Ahh, I thought so in the beginning...« He seemed to tell his fiends and they were curiously looking at Chris. »How is life here under the Jihadists?« Chris wanted to know. His friend shook his head. »They live like the people 1500 years ago. It is terrible. But here in Mosul, they don't enforce their rules on the population so much as it is a a city of 3 million people. And they know they are dependent on the people. So as you see we can smoke among ourselves.« The group became talkative. The goalkeeper recounted. »Iraq is stuck in Chaos for a long time. First Saddam Hussein, then after his death came the Shiites and now Islamic States Sunnis. We are used to chaos and violence.« The group nodded gloomily. »The jihadists forced the Sharia law on us, which is a bad thing. But it's still better than the shiites that were killing the Sunnis.« Another one disagreed. »That means if you are Sunni now, you might be better off... Which most people are here in Mosul. But if you are Shiite now, you are either dead or will be soon.«

Chris wanted to ask more but saw Abu Lot appeared on the pitch. They played another game and went back to the apartment.

Ortega entered the cafe of the Police Department looking for his pal Chad. Chad was a small chubby guy who liked to entertain his colleagues with his comedy. »You know what the sheriff of Missouri said when saw the black kid with 12 gunshots to his head?« The men at the table shook their heads and prepared for a good laugh. »Most terrible suicide I have ever seen!« Laughter erupted among the men. Ortega approached his friend. »Can you come to my office later? I need to talk to you about something.« Chad nodded his head and continued with his story telling.

An hour later Chad knocked at the door and entered his room. »Whassup Bro?« He asked his friend. Ortega waited till he ha closed the door behind him. »Do you have access to the files we gathered on Black Jack? I am on to something there.« Chad was in charge of the evidence room. He grinned conspiratorially. »You know that the case is closed. The FBI took over. Or have I missed something there?« »I know, that's why it's called a favor... Can you help me get the files?« Chad shrugged. He couldn't say no to his friend who had covered him so many times. »Fortunately I still have the files with me. They never picked it up. It's all ther, witness statements, camera videos etc. etc.«

»Thank you buddy.«

They spent the day in the apartment as the encounter with the prisoner was planned after sunset.

Abu Lot was the only one present in the living room liste-ning and Chris joined him. »What is your real name?« He started the conversation. »I'm not allowed to tell you, I'm afraid.« Chris thought of another approach to start the con-versation. »What kind of music did you like before you came here?« Abu Lot smirked. »We are actually encouraged not to talk about our past lives. But...« He looked around and noti-ced that no one was there. »I liked Hip Hop. Good old Gangsta Rap. It's nothing like a gangsta party..« He intoned. Chris laughed. »And do you have brothers and sisters?« »Yes one younger brother. He finished his school and is now in Mallorca with his friends.« He smiled. »And I am here in Iraq.« Chris pondered who he could get to Abu lot the same way the French guy had tried with him. »That reminds me of a story. We were on a trip in Mallorca with some friends from school. One friend of mine was the coolest and funniest lad in class. Everybody liked him. We were his audience and he was always seeking attention. So one day we were at the riffs about 15 meter above the water. There were no people and you could not see who deep the water was. But he wanted to jump. We told him that it was too dangerous but that probably turned him on even more. He told me to record him doing an Auerbach. Although we didn't want him to jump we knew we couldn't stop him. So we thought, all will be fine. He waited for the camera to roll, made steps and jumped down the rock. He completed the Auerbach perfectly. But when he came down, he landed on a pointed rock that rammed through his heart. He was dead instantly.« He looked at Abu Lot. The story was mostly made up but he wanted to make a point. »He was so stubborn! He probably knew it was a bad idea jumping into the blue, but this ego was bigger than his rationale. He didn't want to appear weak and so he jumped into his death.«

At that moment Abu Masala came back with some bags of groceries. He noticed that atmosphere between the two. »What are you talking about?« Chris got up and stretched. »About how we kicked their asses at the game yesterday. We were a good team.« He winked at Abu Lot and then turned around. »I'll take a little nap. Call me when lunch is ready.« Abu Masala watched his brother closely. »You have to be careful with the non-believers. They were sent by the shaitan. I can see that he is trying to get into your head.« Abu

Lot denied that. »Nah, don't worry brother. I'm here with you because we made the right decision.« Abu Masala nodded doubtfully. »Don't worry, I can handle it.« Abu Lot added and gave him a slight pad on the knee.

It was after break of dawn when it was time to go. »It's showdown. Let's bring Koletzki home.« Paulsen said enthusiastically. They got into the pick ups and set out for the encounter with Koletzki.

Chris felt the tension rise as they sped over the highway. He didn't want to imagine how a ‚traitor' was treated in a prison off the Islamic State. But help was on the way. They rode outside of the city until they reached a small hill with an old castle on top. They mounted the hill in the dark and entered the front court of the old crumbly building. In the center of the yard four armed and masked fighters were standing with torches. In front of them was a small chubby man.« Abu Lot greeted the man deferentially. »Salaamaleikum Nasrallah.« The man greeted him and his guests. »Thank you for coming all the way to our state. I hope the journey was not too arduous.« He led them inside. »The German government wants to have one of my black sheep? I hope you came with a good offer.« »Of course, but before we engage in the negotiations we wold like to see Koletzki.« Nasralla made a gesture and two fighters brought the prisoner who was clad in a yellow suit. »The great Abu Hattab!« Abu Masla laughed derisevely. Paulsen ignored Abu Masala. »Mr. Koletzki, we are sent by the German Government.« He adressed him in German. »We want to bring you home to Germany. Is that in your interest?« The man showed no reaction. Paulsen tried again. »Do you want to return home after this?« Koletzki didn't answer. Nasrallah touched him on his shoulder. »You can talk to the non-believers.« For the first time he raised his head and looked at Paulsen. »Bismallah e rahmane rahim. My name is now Abu Hattab. I am a soldier of the Caliphate and I will never return to the land of the Kufar!« Paulsen looked at Nasrallah. Can we have a moment with him alone?« Nasrallah shrugged. »Sure, you can use that room.« When the door closed behind them, Paulsen took a deep breath. »You can trust us, we are here to help you.« The room was lit by a torch and Paulsen could see Koletzki's face. He had dark long hair and a guy beard. He looked meager. »How can I trust you?« Paulsen was relieved that he talked to them. »Your wife Shelley and your daughter died in a car crash the 27th of May 2012. You were freelance journalist and didn't have anything to lose. You went to the Islamic State as a fighter until your true identity had been revealed. Now it's time to go home.« Koletzki nodded his head. »I trust you, There is only one problem. I fell in love with a yesidi woman. If she won't be able to come with me, I'm not going without her.« Chris clapped his hands. »That shouldn't be a problem. Let's get out of here.

They knocked on the door. But nobody opened. Chris knocked again. »Hallo, wc are finished now.« Nothing. Irritated he looked at Paulsen. »Mr. Nasrallah?« No answer. It slowly dawned on them that they had run into a trap.

»Hallo Andrew? I am Adriana Borrero, the court psychiatric in the case of black jack. Can we talk about the incident?«
»Yes, sure.«
Two hours later they faced each other in a student cafe. »Thanks for coming. I talked to Yusuf's mother and she suggested that we meet.« Andrew leaned back. »Yes the way they presented the incident was not how I perceived it. I saw his mother on TV and thought I'd contact her.« Adriana was curious. »So what happened then?« »Andrew drank from his Coke. »Black Jack sat next to me. I observed him get up and move to the side exit. When he opened the door - for a split second - I could see a second person in the lit alley. When he re-entered the hall he threw a smoke grenade so people could not see clearly what was going on. Black Jack had changed his clothes and wore a gas mask. And after he started shooting there was complete chaos.« Andrew shrugged. »What I'm saying is this. They say: he was the only perpetrator and that he went to his car, got the weapons and came back. I say: There was someone waiting outside who had the gear with him and he changed in that alley. It would have taken much longer if he had gone to the parking lot. Conclusion: There might be more than one perpetrator. And I wonder why the police are not following this trail?« Adria-

na took notes. »Ok, easy, easy. So you say, the door opened a crack when he slipped through and you saw what exactly? A whole person, a head, a leg? What was it?« Andrew looked into her cleavage and blushed. »I ah, like I told you, I saw a person.« He got up and indicated the part of the body he saw. »Look, he made that loud noise when he walked down the stairs and I kept staring at his chunky shoes. When he opened the door my eyes where still fixed on his shoes and I saw another shoe. And a leg of course. So there had to be another person.« Adriana nodded slightly. »I mean I mentioned it to the officer I spoke with, but it never was even mentioned anywhere. So I called Mrs. Black Jack to inform her about the fact. That's all.« He looked at Adriana. »And you are 100% sure of that third shoe in the crack?« She couldn't hold back a smile. »Yes Ma'm, that crack was definitely lit.«

Chapter 13

Not far from Sharazad Boulevard and Ali Baba Avenue stood the breathtaking building with the three minarets, four cupolas and colorful arches. An ambience of 1001 nights.But the arabesque building was not to be found in Damascus or Baghdad but in Opa-locka.

The muslim congregation celebrated its Eid al-Fitr, the holiest islamic holiday marking the end of fasting. Comparable with Easter for the Christians. Respectively a lot of muslims had come to the mosque, like Luis. He belonged to the growing number of muslim Latinos. Similar to the Adr-americans in the 60s now also the latinos discovered their historic and cultural connections to the Islam and the arabic world. Someone had told Chris that there were more than 4000 spanische words derived from the arabic language. Among them all words beginning will al like almohads and alcalde. Especially for Cubans who were not allowed to have an religion during Communism, Islam in fashion. The specialty this year was that the holiday clashed with 9.11. which was a national day of mourning. The imam of the congregation was therefore went to great lengths to set themselves apart from the Islamists. The mosque was packed.

»Hola amigo, Como vas?« His friend Carlos from Puerto Rico greeted Luis. »You want to hear something funny? When I came here there was an old woman in front of the mosque. As she was standing alone I asked if she needed help. And she shot back. No, thank you. You people are celebrating 9/11, and the deaths of thousands of people. You should be ashamed.« He shook his head. »They don't seem to understand that it is a coincidence that those dates came together.« Luis answered. The atmosphere in Miami had become tense after the gun ban and the anger was especially directed towards muslims. But now was not the time to have negative feelings.

The Imam wanted to begin. The middle-aged man from the Maghreb wore a white Djelleba whose hood was elaborately pulled over the head. He watched his congregation and started to preach. Dear brothers.Today is a sad and a happy day indeed. The day of 9/11 will always be in the American conscience as the day of terror. These attacks were terrible and 100% unislamic. Islam is a peaceful religion that brings people together and not one to divide. I only have to look at this colorful congregation to know we are one. Black, white, latino, arab and we even have a yellow man.« The congregation chuckled. But the imam turned serious again. »The terrorists besmirch our religion. It is for them that the Islam has a bad reputation. Whenever you hear a brother defend these terrible attacks or talk like them, don't sit and do nothing. We have to stand up for our religion and protect it from these radicals. And bring the brother back to the peaceful Islam.« Some men shouted Allahu'Akbar. »And I have another concern. Whenever people who are not muslims talk bad about our religion, do the same thing. Defend the Islam. But if you sense that they are not interested in a discussion but only want to provoke a bad reaction, then leave them alone. I know that might sound weak to some, and it is hard to walk away if someone is provoking you. But in reality it shows strength. You don't immerse in negativity. Let those negative people have negative thoughts. But we stay out of this game.« The imam looked in the faces of the young men. He knew that a lot of them came from the streets and it was not in their blood to walk away from trouble. But they wouldn't be here if they didn't want to change their lives. »Try this exercise, and it will be easier every time. Remember. You don't have to prove yourself to no-one but god!« The imam paused. From outside voices could be heard. Suddenly the window glass broke and a stone landed not far from the Imam. No one moved and looked at the stone. »Come outside, You muslim pigs.« Someone shouted. »We slaughter you like pigs and send you to paradise.« Another one yelled. The congregation became agitated. The imam realized that it was about to get ugly. »Lock the doors. They want to provoke us, but we stay here. Luis and his friend changed a look. A moment later a burning ball of paper came flying through the hole. That was too much. Panic and anger erupted like a volcano. About 20 young men stormed outside and started to fight as they had learnt on the streets of Opa-locka. Luis was blind of rage and punched at everybody in his way. Although the police came fast, they couldn't stop the fight. As soon as they had arrested some people, another fight broke loose at the other end. After about half an hour though, most of the people were arrested. Among them Luis.

They took the blankets that were lying around and sat around the torch that was almost burnt down. Nobody had said a word in a while. »What are you thinking?« Chris asked Paulsen. »I didn't see that coming.« He said gloomily. »And frankly, I don't know, what prompted his decision. Prisoner exchanges are a vital source of income for the Islamic State. If anything happens to us, the German government will never negotiate again. So I really don't know what is going on.« Koletzki shook his head. »You don't seem to understand the rationale of the Islamic State. Because they don't have one. They are a bad business partner, if you ask me.« He looked at Chris. »I'm sorry to be the reason why you are here.« Silence set in again, which made Chris uncomfortable. »You were here for 5 years. Did you ever plan to return to Germany? It mentioned that you have. A wife now...« Koletzki laughed. »Initially I had planned to stay only for 6 months until I had my story and then go back. I was like you. Young and motivated. But it didn't turn out as expected. For one part they take your passports and build a system of controls that makes it difficult for fighters to escape. But what I also underestimated was how they get to your

87

head. I thought I'd be Odysseus who would resist the sirens. But I am not.« He laughed a disillusioned laugh. »You live with your brothers 24/7 and inevitably start to grow a bond. You live through extraordinary moments that have a psychological effect. I mean, if someone saves your life, you will feel some attachment to this person. And you hear the ideology over and over again until you start to believe it. In the beginning the voice of reason is loud and keeps reminding you what is wrong and what is right. But that voice gets weaker and weaker with time and simply drowned out by the voices of your brothers telling you what is right and what is wrong. And the boundaries change.« He grabbed for a bottle of water and took a sip, only to realize that it was empty. Frustrated he threw it at against the door. Unregarding Chris kept digging. »What happened then? How did you end up prisoner?« Koletzki rolled his eyes as one does relating from memory. »One day my brothers and I went to a slave market in Raqqa where fighters could buy captured Yesidi women. A tall blonde with green eyes caught my eye at once. Her name was Elena. She was reminding me of my late wife. And her face was filled with horror as the women were pushed in the center of the room and the brothers were bargaining for them. Like on a bazaar. Only with more passion. As the brothers were yelling and arguing I noticed Elena fixating me with her green eyes. I don't know what she did with me, but when it was her turn, I did my best to ensure that I gave the highest bid. And I bought her.« Koletzki had wet eyes. »She moved in and I treated her like my ex wife and not like a slave. We fell in love she helped me find my voice of reason again. We made plans to escape from Dawla Islamiya. But shortly before we could flee, I was betrayed by a brother.« He looked at the dwindling flame. »The brother who betrayed me was Abu Masala.«

»Asalaalmalaikum Jed.« Nasrallah spoke to him from a secure line. »I have thought about what you said the other day about cutting the funding. And I must say I didn't like that at all. If Dawla Islamiya is not good enough for the purposes of the CIA then it is better to say so openly.« »Nasrallah, calm down...« Jed tried to interrupt, but the Iraqi kept talking. »No, you listen to me. You need us more than we need you. If Dawla Islamiya goes down, so be it. Our fighters are ready to die for the Caliphate!« He bristled with anger. »We don't need your Cyborgs anymore. So I just wanted to inform you, that we have 40 foreign prisoners right now. And that there will be no negotiations but executions.« He hung up the phone. Jed Collins stared incredulously at the phone.

Chapter 14

»Where am I?« Chubbs opened his eyes. Was it a bad dream or was he really beat down the night before. He couldn't remember. I only drank half a bottle of Rum, he wondered. He scanned his surroundings and came to the conclusion that he was in a hospital room. What had happened? To his relieve in this moment a doctor entered the room. » Good morning, How do you feel.« He asked looking over the brink of his glasses. »Doctor, I don't know what happened. I think I was beat down and I from then on I know nothing.« Chubbs explained agitatedly. The doctor made a gesture to calm down. »You were brought here last night without consciousness from the canalization. We fixed your wounds and gave you something to sleep. Now, you are free to go if you want.« He looked at Chubbs pensively. »But to be honest I would not recommend that. That was probably a wake up call yesterday. You should change something before it's to late. Do you hear me?« Chubbs nodded groggily. »We have a program here for people in your situation called CoC or Continuum of Care. I recommend that you enroll in that program.« Chubbs rubbed his swollen face. Usually he didn't like these programs, because he needed his alcohol. But the doctor was right. Maybe that was a wake up call. »In this non governmental program we help you get off drugs and alcohol. We help you rediscover your strengths and at the end

of the program even grant a few of the applicants an opportunity to work abroad. The program is free and takes 12
months. Does that sound appealing to you?« The doctor
gave him a big smile. Chubby joined in. »Yes that sounds
good. Thank you so much.

Adriana opened the door and greeted Ortega with kiss on
the cheek. »Thank you for coming.« Ortega kept her in her
arms. »How is your brother? Is he alright?« Luis had been
kept in custody after the incident in front of the mosque. She
detested violence and was appalled to hear about her brother's involvement. But when he told her the whole story she
could imagine how the situation could escalate and didn't
blame the young men. And the most important thing: no one
of neither side was seriously hurt. »Aside from a strained
wrist and a blue eye he is fine.« She answered. The incident
in Opa-locka was one of many escalations against muslims,
that many had feared. From the kitchen a delicious smell
came forth. »What are you cooking? It's mouth-watering.«
Ortega asked. »You'll see in a minute. Sit down in the living
room and let me prepare everything.«
Ortega said hallo to grandma and Santo. He had a hang for
kids and didn't mind having them around. He felt more and
more that he wanted a relationship but he didn't want to
press Adriana. »Vienen a comer!« Adriana shouted and Santo was the first to jump. »We have Ajiaco Bayames and Bo-

cadito, in company with a redline from the Florida region.«
She announced dressed in an apron and made an exaggera-
ted curtsy like a servant. He couldn't avert his eyes from her.
She took off the apron and displayed a sexy black dress underneath. Ortega was stunned by her beauty. She sat down.
»Today is a special day. It is 2 years now, that my beloved
husband Jake is dead.« She made a cross. »Maybe he looks
down on us and from above and is happy that his good friend is taking care of us.« She raised her glass and looked Ortega deep in his eyes. »Now let's begin, before the food gets
cold.« Ortega tried the first spoon of the soup and was wo-
wed. »You have to give me the receipe!« He exclaimed.
»That doesn't mean I can cook, but at least I know what I'm
talking about.« Adriana laughed and nodded at her mother
to tell him. »Ajiaco is a cuban soup from Bayanes.«, her mother explained. »There are different kind of Ajiacos according to the regions. But this is Ajaco from Bayamo. That's a
city in the cuban province Granma. And it's the city where
my husband and I were born and have lived before we came
to Miami. It's filled with beef and pork, corn, white malanga,
yellow malanga, name, green and ripe plantains, cassava
and sweet potatoes. And it is seasoned with Chili, onion, gar-
lic, salt and lemon.« »It's power food. Good for your
muscles.« Adriana added and winked. »I told you that I
move in tonight, right?« Ortega joked. Adriana liked his
lightheartedness and his humor. But he could be tough too.
That was probably the reason why she had a history with

cops. After dinner they played a little bit with Santo until he had to go to bed.

Then they finally had time for their own. Adriana told Ortega what she had learned from the meeting with Andrew and that she supposed that there might have been a second perpetrator or at least someone who helped. Ortega revealed a memory stick and connected it to the lap top. »I will show you something. This is the video from the surveillance Camera. Unfortunately it doesn't cover the emergency exit aisle, but at least this.« He started the video. You could see the people entering the hall. Adriana recognized Andrew with his girl and next to him Black Jack. He forwarded the video to the moment when Black jack got up and walked down the side aisle. The door opened and he paused the video at the exact moment when the door was opened. The angle of the camera was apparently broader than Andrew's view. Because in plain view there was a second man standing in the door. Adriana choked. Andrew was right. She changed a look with Ortega. This was a game changer. »This is bigger than we thought.« She uttered slowly. Ortega nodded. »We now know for a fact that the FBI is ignoring important evidence.« He enlarged the fuzzy picture of the second man who seemed to be caucasian. »We don't know who the man is and on whose behalf he was acting. But we have to be aware that it can be dangerous to do research on our own.« Adriana nodded. She involuntary thought of Yusuf's mother who was devastated. She knew she had to do everything she could to

93

find out what really happened. Adriana closed the lap top and sighed. »I will go to visit a friend of Yusuf in Colorado. Maybe he can tell me more.« Ortega took her into his arms and came close to her lips. »You can't go alone. I will accompany you.« »Really? You do that for me?« She whispered. Instead of a response Ortega gave her a kiss. She returned the kiss, but then retracted and looked away. »It's late, it's better we talk tomorrow.« Ortega was obviously disappointed, but said nothing. Without saying a word he got up and went for the door. Adriana got hold of him shortly before he reached the door. »I'm so sorry. I'm really sorry.« Ortega paused without turning back. Then he slammed the door and left.

Adriana finished the bottle of red wine before she went to sleep. In her dream she called Jason to come by. She needed to talk to him. Jason rang at the door. Both of them stared at each other in silence. Then suddenly Jason began laughing real hard. He hugged her and gave her a kiss on the cheek. Then he turned around and headed for the dark. Adriana suddenly felt relieved.

Chapter 15

Abu Lot had asked for an appointment with Nasrallah. Abu Masala had played his role as the media chief well, but in reality Abu Lot was the one in charge. They used this strategy to protect their best men. »I wanted to discuss the situation of the Germans with you.« He began, when he had sat down. »No, there is nothing to discuss.« Nasrallah answered, looking out of the window. »The emir has made his decision. And he is right, like always. We are going to set an example and kill all of our western prisoners in one major event. That way our enemies will be reminded who they are dealing with.« Abu Lot didn't want to give up that easily. »As chief of media I have to warn of the dire consequences. That decision will damage us more than help us. Ransom for Prisoners are a significant part of our income. No state will ever negotiate with us again.« Nasrallah laughed. »Abu Lot, you are an able man. But there are things, that you don't understand. We agree we can't let go Abu Hattab. He knows the inner circle and simply is a risk. But the reason we need to kill all prisoners is to demonstrate strength to our followers. In times where the whole world is against us, we show that we fight like lions. The decision of the emir is set. The beheadings will take place on friday. The emir expects you to film it and show it to the world.« Abu Lot bit his tongue, he didn't know what to say. The death penalty was ruled. There was no way to alter the decision of the emir. Nasrallah dismissed Abu Lot. But he had no intention to leave. »With all due respect, I have to tell you that I don't agree with that decision! It may be true that the hardliners will applaud that measure, but it was you yourself who told me that as chief of media you have to think sensible and how effects turn out in the long run.« Nasrallah held up his hand and Abu Lot stopped talking. »You might be right, Abu Lot. But listen. The emir told me a long time ago that he wanted to quit demanding ransom like a group of criminals. He said it is not worthy of Dawla Islamiya to act like that. So he told me about his plan to end it. And now the time has come to elevate. Now tell me. Do you question the Emir's ability to lead?« Abu Lot shook his head vehemently. »No brother. I trust the wisdom of the emir. I just want Dawla islamiya to thrive and grow.« Nasrallah put a hand on the shoulder. »I know that, Abu Lot. That is why I chose you for this position.«

»Violent crackdown of protests!«, read the headline of the Herald Tribune. Adriana had taken some days off and booked a flight to Colorado Springs. Except for Ortega no one knew what she was doing. She had found and contacted Yusuf's former roommate, Jake Riley. She had played the authority card and had not given him much of a choice. On the six hour flight she read about the new developments in the country. The transitory gun ban divided the country and tensions seemed to intensify. Demonstrations flared up all over the country and police measures tightened. The US was at the brink of a civil war. Especially in New York and L.A. the protests had become out of control and the police needed support from the army. Their tactic was intimidation. It sent shivers down her spine. She put the newspaper aside and watched the rockies. From up here everything looked so peaceful. But down there something bad was brewing.

She took a photo of Santo out of her purse and watched it. It instantly gave her a pleasant feeling and she smiled. Next to that was a picture of her parents, who were holding her in their arms. Her father looked young and neat in that photo, which was taken when they were about one year in Miami. He had a melancholic look on his face as he gazed at his baby. Adriana choked. The couple could afford only a small apartment in Hialeah, although her father sacrificed himself for the family. He worked as a day laborer and came home exhausted. At night he left the house again. Her mother told her later that he had had a drinking problem. The American dream had turned out to be a disappointment, frustration and shame. But he loved his little family and so he carried on without regard for his health. It was Memorial Day when he died. Her mother had told her he had driven to the MacArthur Causeway, had stopped at the parking lane, stepped over the barrier and jumped from the bridge.

Chapter 16

Abu Lot was heading home pondering about the conversation he had with Nasrallah. He barely greeted Abu Masala and sat down next to him on the sofa chewing nervously on his wooden stick. Abu Masala looked at him irritated. »Is Something wrong?« Abu Lot shook his head but didn't answer. Right away After a moment he asked. »Do you remember when we first met in the muslim congregation in Solingen? There was this Imam who told us about how the Quoran has all answers to life and how it had to interpreted into our times. He warned us that the holy book sometimes contained contradictions and how to handle those. He said: Follow the spirit of the holy book! It has to bee seen in the light of passion and love. A good muslim stands out by his altruism, rather than his selfishness, by his reservation rather than his vanity and by his amiability rather than bellicosity.« Abu Masala interrupted him. »Achi, what are you talking? I remember the Imam, and I also know, that he showed us the washed out version of the Islam, the suppressed version. This Imam was a Kufar who tried to lead us astray from the real Islam. We learnt all that. Do you doubt the emir or why do you bring that up now?« Abu Lot shook his head. »No, the word of the emir is the truth and nothing but the truth.« He hesitated. »But he is human, and humans make mistakes.« He suddenly stood up. »Have you never thought what if we were wrong. What if Mohamed was merciful instead of belligerent?« Abu Maslala grew louder. »I will not do a quern lesson now. If you are doubting the interpretation of the Emir, you might not be fit for your position. Ya ne, we are the founder of this movement that will return to the powerful and mighty Islam of old times. We have a responsibility to our muslim brothers. Maybe the German got into your head. I knew from the beginning, that he is dangerous. Now, he won't be going on our nerves any longer!« He laughed. Abu Lot nodded pensively. »Maybe you are right and he got to me. Thank you for your words, brother.« He gently padded his friend's shoulder. »No worries, I will tell nobody. It happens to the best of us. Shaitan sends the devil to test our believe. But we are stronger!« »Yes, that's true.« Abu Lot answered absent-mindedly. He looked at his friend for a moment and said. »I go to the store because I haven't eaten tonight. Do you want anything?« Abu Masala shot back. »Those cookies with chocolate inside would be nice.« Abu Lot laughed and winked at him.

Adriana cursed inside when she saw the bill of the car rent. The costs kept growing but she dispelled the thought by remembering the desperate face of Sara. She had to find out what really happened.

The City at the foot of Pikes Peak seemed quiet and dozy in the afternoon sun. But she knew that the appearance was deceiving. Several Universities and military bases were located in Colorado Springs, so a lot of young people were living in the city. She freshened up at the hotel and then went to the meeting place where Jake was already waiting. It was a Burger place in the student area. Adriana held up the phone with the picture he had sent her in order to find him. He sat in the back and waved her. A curly ginger guy with thick glasses and a UCCS sweater grinned at her. »Jake?« »Yeah, that would be me.« He awkwardly stood up and shook hands. His puzzled look betrayed that he didn't picture a court psychiatrist look so stunning. He became more irritated when she ordered a double cheeseburger and a beer. »It was a long flight.« She winked at him. »And I'm on vacation, officially.« Then she directed the conversation to the topic she had come for. »You were a friend of Yusuf Zaidi. How well did you know him?« Jake leaned back in his sest. »We shared a room on campus for a whole semester. And we got along just brilliantly from the moment he moved in. He was a funny nerd.« He laughed. »Did you also study neuro sciences?« Jake looked at the cleavage of Adriana, and blushed when she noticed it. »Ahhm Yes that is the reason we got along so well.« The drinks were served and Adriana took a big sip smirking. »So, what do you think of what happened in Miami? Did you see that coming?« »No, not at all. We were all shocked, when we heard it was him.« Jake shot back indignantly. »I mean, Yusuf, a jihadist? That was not how we knew him. You know, whenever religion came up he used to say: If the followers of a religion really strived to act on behalf of the founders of their religions, then there would be no animosity between followers of different religions. That was Yusuf.« Adriana nodded. »His mother mentioned that he had changed when the program started. Can you tell me how you perceived that. »Yeah, with time you realized that he was stressed. He was barely at home and if then only to sleep. I thought he was just overworked and let him alone. One day he had packed his suitcase and told me he would move to Fort Carson to do research.« He paused when the waitress served the food. Adriana took a big bite from the burger. »What do you know about the program?«, she asked with a full mouth. Jake looked at her irritated and slowly ate from his salad. »Only what Yusuf told me. It's an assessment course for the PhD program for brain sciences and mind sciences. Students apply as test persons and get 2,400 Dollars. He was accepted. That's all I really know.« Adriana waited for the waitress to put down the new beer. Then she said. »You don't know of any Muslim friends of his? Or maybe some calls?« Jake shook his head. »Ok, then the only cue we have is the program. We need to see what is happening there.« She looked at him hauntingly. »Do you know anyone taking part in that program? »No, unfortunately not.« Jake shot back. »Can you apply for this program?« Jake choked his Coke. »Technically yes. Everybody under 30 can apply.« Adriana was satisfied. »Good, will you do it for your friend? To find out what really happened?« Jake wavered. »Well if you really think the program has something to do with his decision to do the attack? I don't think so. But I actually can use the money. Ok I'm in.«

Back in the hotel, she called Ortega and told him about her plan. He was not enthusiastic. »I have a bad feeling having you pry about on your own. That's not a joke baby.« He wasn't meant to say baby, but it just had slipped. »I will come and help you. Don't do anything stupid until I'm there!«

Adriana felt relieved. She felt much safer when Ortega was around.

Abu Lot got into the car and rode through the streets without aimlessly. He thought of the last conversation with his mother. She had told him that his brother had passed his A-levels and with the money he had earns as barkeeper we was going to Mallorca with his friends. He had to smirk. His little brother in Mallorca and he in the Islamic state. As kids he had taken care of his little brother and he wondered if he was disappointed by him. He hoped that his brother would not follow the same path. Life as a fighter was hard and once you were in it was almost impossible to get out. He only now realized that he was on his way to the old castle, where the Germans were held prisoners. He brought the car to a stop in front of the castle and turned the rearview mirror, so that he could look at this face. It had been a while since he really had looked at his face although he washed it every day several times before prayer. But vanity was a sin and within his brothers there was this dynamic that here everybody wanted to be the most pious. He scrutinized the little wrinkles on his forehead and around his mouth. His features had turned hard. The furrows of a warrior. He turned the mirror away and prayed. Then he checked his gun belt, took the Kalashnikov and got out of the car. He hesitated a moment as if to receive the go ahead. Then he marched off.

Chris had given up trying to find some sleep. He leaned against the wall of the small, scant room that was now only lit by a little candle that they had found. The cold crept inside through the permeable walls. He embraced his legs with his arms and rocked forth and back. His mind was racing. He had taken the decision to come here by himself. Like Koletzki he had risked it all. He wondered what would be his legacy after his death. Besides his parents there were not many people that would truly mourn, he pictured. Most friendships were superficial and his liaisons short lived. He sighed with pain. He had always tried to go his own way, but in the end given in to the social norms. »Why are you here?« He asked Paulsen who was also awake. »Because I have a family to sustain.« He saw the desperation in Chris'e eyes. »And because I get satisfaction from my work helping people.« Chris nodded. He looked over to Koletzki who was sound asleep. »Paulsen?« »Yes?« »When we get home, can I visit you and your family? We will laugh about this night then, right?« »Yes Chris, for sure. My kids will love you.« Chris knew that Paulsen had a smile on his face.

»There is an application process for the program«, Jake explained as they were strolling through the campus. They sat down at a little pond seamed with conifers. »Good, I can prep you for that. When can you start?« She winked at Jake. He blushed at the thought of spending some preparation time with Adriana. »Yeah It's really hard to get in. I definitely need some preparation.« He mumbled distractedly. »The next program starts in two weeks time.« He read from the brochure he was given. The leading professor would be a Prof. Marvin Fitzek. He was well known at the university but he had never had a course with him so far. There was an image of a blue brain shelled by red arrows. He wondered if the program could possibly have something to do with the attack. He doubted it. But aside from the money he would also receive credits and on top of that he would spend some quality time with Adriana.

Chapter 17

Abu Lot had to wait a moment until his eyes were used to the pitch black darkness.. He climbed the back of the hill until he reached a spot about 10 meters above the old castle. From here he had a good view. When they had left the castle, there had been 4 guards. 2 were in the hallway in front of the room and 2 walked up and down the castle. From his position he could see the lights of the flashlights oscillating back and forth behind the ruins. He waited a moment. »Let's go.« He crept downhill. At a broken part of the ruins he kneeled down to take a rest. Besides from the distant noises from the streets it was deadly silent. He wrapped his silk scarf around his head, so that only his eyes could be seen.

Then he stepped over the ruins. Creeping up, slowly, like a panther from behind to the prey, the source of light. A breath of air for every step. Heart pumping. Looking around the corner. The guard only 4 steps away. He kneels down and pulls out his knife from his fanny pack. He knows he only has one try. The victim must not utter a sound. His target now two steps away. He closes his eyes. »Allah Akbar. Help your warrior, do the right thing.« In a split second he jumps at the guard that is standing with his back towards him and pulls the knife across his throat. There is a short death rattle, but the vocal chord is severed. The brother collapses. A second blow seals his fate. Abu Lot takes the lamp and walks around the castle, where the second source of light is. He walks up to the guard fast. The man turns around and illuminates him. Clad in his silk scarf he doesn't notice anything. In Arabic the man says: »It's so cold, do you have gloves?« Abu Lot comes close, blinds him with his flashlight and his knife clenched in his fist behind his back. »No I'm afraid not.« He drags his knife and thrusts it across his opponent's throat with a pointed backhand. Again that same the death rattling sound. He cleans the knife on the pants of the fighter then pulls the body to the edge of the wall. He takes the Kalashnikov from his back, loads it and walks to the main entrance. Peeking inside he recognizes the outline of two persons in the light of the torch. One person sitting the other standing next to him. One, two, three fast steps into the center of the room, then a rapid gun fire, a volley from the left to the right and back. Death rattle. Single gun shot. Silence.

»Ortega and Chad?«, Adriana exclaimed in surprise as they entered her hotel room. »Hi sweetie.« Chad gave her a hug after Ortega. »I heard, you want to save the world, so I had some vacation left and thought I might join you.« Relieved she introduced them to Jake. »These are my friends, Ortega and Chad from the Miami police department.« They sat down and discussed their approach. Ortega handed Jake an old silver watch. »It has a bug inside so that we can eavesdrop. That means if something seems odd to you, say it out loud.« Ortega noticed Jake becoming nervous. »Whenever you want to quit, tell us, and we come in and get you out. We are well equipped, I assure you.«

Chris startled when he heard the gun shots. All of the men instantly were awake and prepared for the worst. Then another shot. A moment later they heard a key in the lock and a black clad man stood in front of them. The stress was imbearable. »Don't worry it's me.« Abu Lot pulled off his scarf. »The Emir has sentenced you to death. That's why I am here to free you.« Chris jumped up and gave him a hug. Abu Lot also hugged Abu Hattab. »Your name is Koletzki now? Good to know.« »Thank you brother, Allah may reward you for this a thousand times.« He took off the yellow jumpsuit and took a combat gear of one of the guards. Paulsen did the same thing. Chris already looked like a fighter. They covered their faces and took up the kalashnikovs and flashlights of the guards. They now looked like a death squad. Paulsen asked Abu Lot for his phone. »I can make a call and they blow up this place in minute. That way they think we are dead and we might gain some time.« He took the phone and ordered a drone. »In 15 minutes it will blow up. So let's get out of here.« »Follow me to the car.« Abu Lot told them. They went down the hill which was illuminated by the street

107

lights. When they reached the car Koletzki hesitated. »I have to get my wife. I don't leave her behind.« Paulsen agreed. »We don't separate. We go pick your woman together.« Abu Lot sat in front and started the engine. The white pick up opened his eyes and set in motion. »Abu Hattab, Sorry I mean Koletzki, you have to call your wife, she is in great danger now.« Abu Lot urged him. Koletzki took the phone and punched in the numbers. After the third ring a voice answered at the other end. »Michael, Is that you?« She had a secure number that only he knew. »Yes Darling, It's me.« Her voice trembled. »Listen, I escaped with the help of some friends. We have to get out as soon as possible! You are in danger. Let's meet at the place where we used to pluck cherries. Hurry. See you there. I Love you.« He ended the call before she could respond. »Plucking cherries?« Chris laughed. Koletzki told Abu Lot the new adress in arabic then he turned to Chris. »I had an apartment in the city. But Abu Lot knows how it is, there is no privacy among your brothers. So I bought a house on the outskirts of Mosul and renovated it. When I was married with Elena we planned or escape there. I somebody asked where I was going I used to tell them I was plucking cherries with my slave. That way everybody knew what I meant and didn't ask further. Chris couldn't hold back a smile. But Paulsen frowned. »And you are sure, that nobody knows about this house?« »I took some precautions and I didn't tell anyone. I am pretty sure that nobody knows. At least we win some time.« It was a pitch black night and they were the only car on the highway. According to the lights there were only a few houses. They left the highway and turned into a small street, that was more an tarred path and shortly after reached a little house surrounded by a high stone wall. In the gateway stood a blue Volvo. »Elena has already arrived!« Lokelzki shouted out excitedly. The house was illuminated by the car lights. No visible movement, no audible sound. All quiet. Was it a trap? »I go first«, Koletzki said. »If everything is ok, I'll get you. Abu Lot and Paulsen readied their guns when Koletzki approached the house. Abu Lot put in the reverse gear. Koletzki stood in front of the door. It took some moments until the door was opened. In the car lights appeared a woman with long, blonde hair. She suppressed a cry of joy and hugged Koletzki intimately. Relieved they stored their weapons away and got out of the car. They didn't have much time until their enemies would figure out where the have been hiding.

When they united in the main room, Paulsen asked Abu Lot for his phone. He dialed his number and waited. »It's me again, Paulsen.« He muttered a code. »Please locate this phone and send a helicopter to rescue 5 people. As fast as possible. Thank you.« Everybody was watching him closely. Then he got the thumbs up. »They located us. Now all we can do is wait.« Relieved the group hugged each other and laughed. Except for Abu Lot. »I wish you all the best, but I won't accompany you. I have to get going somewhere else.«

»What? Come again?« Chris exclaimed incredulously. »You come with us! You can start a new life. See your family.« He tried to convince his friend. »No, I have blood on my hands, they would send me to prison for a long time. When I came here I knew that this would be my last station.« He looked at Koletzki. »And besides, I need to talk to someone. He addressed Chris. »Pleas tell my mother that I'm sorry. I didn't want to hurt anybody, I just wanted a chance in life. And the Islamic State offered that chance. I now know how they made it. But then I was a stupid follower. I just hope, that I at least did some good by helping you escape so that the world will know what the Islamic State is really about.« He gave Chris a hug. Then Koletzki and said goodbye to the others. With his dancing and non-chalant stride he walked off into the dark night. Chris became deeply sad, because he knew he would never see his friend.

The Colorado Springs Psychiatric Rehabilitation Center was 20 minutes from the city and surrounded by open fields. The huge building complex of red brick stones and white windowsills and a gothic white cupola rose up high in the grey sky. »Good morning, Ladies and Gentlemen.« Prof. Greeted the participants of the program, who had assembled at a separated part of the University psychiatry. The professor was a little man with scarce hair, but unusual presence. »From hundreds of applicants from all over the country we chose you. You will have the pleasure to take part in and learn the latest techniques on brain sciences.« Jake cast a glance at the group. There were two faces he had seen before on campus. The rest he had never seen before. Next to him were a Rastafari. He sat comfortably in his chair with a wide smile. Jake scented a trace of marihuana. He has a altered state of consciousness already.« He thought.

»The program is certified by the State«, the professor continued. »That means that all substances used in this program are specifically produced for scientific research purposes.« He looked at the group amused. »That is to say best quality.« The Rastafarian laughed the loudest. »You can quit the program any minute, in case you get the feeling that it is to demanding. But I encourage you to hang on till the end in order to get to know your limits and the human brain. I can assure you that it will be an interesting journey.« He looked at the Rastafarian. »And if you have arrived in Disneyland, say hello to Micky from me.« He winked. The Professor knew there were people who only took part in order to try psychedelic drugs for free. But these people were often disappointed. The program consisted of lengthy and tiring tests that brought the participants to their limit. Psychologically and physically. But once in a while he was surprised by some of them.

After the introduction they stood outside and talking. Jake approached the rasta. »Hi I never saw you on campus. Where are you coming from?« He eyed up Jake and scratched his head: »That's a good question, I think I am inscribed in Harlem but I can't tell you for sure.« Jake didn't know if he was joking or not. Yet he snickered. »Nah, I'm pulling your leg. My name is Malcom. I study psychology at the NYU and I'm interested in the brain - like the rest of us, I imagine.« He stated eloquently. And Prof. Dr. Fitzek is a distinguished expert in this field, as you know. Jake hesitated for a moment. He wondered how Malcom could afford the tuition fee. But instead he spluttered. »Yes the topic is quite exciting. A friend of mine had taken part and he was thrilled how much you learn about yourself. A lasting experience.« He smiled at Malcom nervously. Adriana and Ortega who listened from the van changed a worried look. Malcom standing with his legs apart and hands in his hips stared penetratingly into his eyes. »Are you always so fidgety? You should smoke Reefa once in a while. Or is it because you have never seen a big fat Rasta?« Jake flinched. »Nonsense. I have some black friends! There was one on my ice hockey team.« Malcom laughed. »A nigga playing ice hockey? I wanna get to know this brother? But you said he was on your team - what happened? Did they chase him away throwing bananas or what? Or he changed to the basketball team?« Jake grew more and more irritated. If this big fat Rasta though he could provoke him, he was wrong. Because he could also get into peoples' head. »You know, what is the worst word you can say to a black man? Starting with N and ending with R?« -

»Nigger?« »No neighbor!« Pahh there he went. Malcom stepped closer to Jake. »And do you know why the white man flew on the moon? - Because he had heard that the Indians had owned land there!« They stood nose to nose and talked in a loud voice so that other participants turned around to look at them. Jake noticed it. What if the program had already started and this was part it. He turned around and threw his hands up in a theatrical way. »If you want to provoke me, I gotta tell you. I will not argue with you at that level.« Satisfied he looked at the group and then to Malcom. But he felt provoked so he added. »But as you brought up cliches. What is the most depressing day in Harlem?« Certain of victory he faced the crowd. -»Father's day!«

My name is Charles Norton, nickname Chubbs. I am 55 years old born in Houston, Texas.« He disclosed to an assistant sitting opposite of him in a sterile room. At the age of 5 my family moved to Miami. May parents, my little sister Suzie-Anne and I. My father was an alcoholic and abused my mother and us on a daily basis. He punched her so hard that she had to go to hospital several times. But she always returned to him. Probably she really loved him. When I was 12 he passed away. He died of a heart attack. Shortly after another man moved in with us. In the beginning he was nice to us. But he did drugs. And when he was high he was a mean person. It was almost as bad as with my real dad. Some day a

113

friend of mine told me: »Hey try this, you will feel like you are in heaven.« I did and got addicted to crack cocaine.« The assistant frowned but kept taking notes. »My mother didn't make it to separate her from this evil man. At the age of 14 I couldn't bear it anymore and told my mother: either him or me. She chose him and I left. In the beginning I stayed with friends and had at least a roof over my head. But soon I found kids that were in the same position or worse. We occupied desolated houses and apartments. That was the beginning of my life on the streets.« He followed the look of the assistant and showed his arm. »The cuts on my arm? Yeah I cut myself as a way to turn my emotional pain into physical pain that can be controlled. Sometimes up to a hundred cuts. But there is a point where the cuts don't help you anymore. You just want it to end. I tried to end it many times.« He paused for a moment. »But then I got to know Caren. She encouraged me and helped me get off the drugs. I found a job and we had an apartment together. It was the best time of my life. It didn't last long though. My sister Suzie-Anne died giving birth to her child. I was so devastated that I resorted to drugs again. I lost my job and the apartment. And after a while also Caren.« He shook his head. »I reached the point: If I survive this day, good. If not, it doesn't really matter. Nobody will miss me.«

Chapter 18

It had been almost two hours after he left the apartment, to get cookies. He hoped that it was not too late. He drove to the house of Nasrallah. Only the most trusted brothers knew his private adress. Abu Lot had gained that trust as a fighter from the first hour. When he arrived the usual three guards were standing in front of the door. He got out and approached them. Although they recognized him, they stopped Abu Lot. »Achi, I have important information for Nasrallah. The explosion was a distraction. A trap.« He took off his gun belt and pushed the youngest aside. »It's a life and death situation. I don't have time for this now.« The young fighter looked at his peers undecided. They shrugged and let him pass. With long strides Abu Lot hurried to Nasrallah's room.

When he entered Nasrallah stood at the exact same spot at the window like the last time. Abu Lot breathed in deeply then closed the door behind him. »I heard you have news? What is so urgent?« »Yes indeed, it is important. And it's a personal thing.« Nasrallah noticed the defiant tone in his brother's voice and became alert. ABu Lot lifted his Jacket and displayed the suicide belt. »But only if you have time.« He clenched the trigger. Dumbfounded Nasrallah sat down in his chair and gestured Abu Lot to also sit down. »You are also a betrayer, Brutus?« Nasrallah sighed disappointedly. Abu Lot ignored it. »Do you remember when we first met in

Alexandria?«, he began. »I had been there for one year at the university with my brothers and we were eager to learn and naive. And then you came along. You had the reputation of knowing secrets about the Islam, that were suppressed by the west and you therefore lived in constant danger. For that reason all meetings were secret. That made it even more attractive for us. A nice move, I have to admit as Media Chief.« While he was speaking he had one hand on the trigger.

Nasrallah tried to assuage him. »Abu Lot, you were valuable to me from the beginning, because you questioned things and always had an independent mind. And I actually thought about what you told me regarding the prisoners and I spoke with the emir about it. He wants to release them...« Abu Lot interrupted him. »Stop it! You won't manipulate me again! The Germans are dead!« His voice was sharp as a butcher's knife. »I realize now, how you used us, creating an exotic and secretive atmosphere and disclosing these nix of old and radical ideas to us. Easy to understand even for the weakest minds searching for simple solutions. The good and the bad. No a particularly new concept.« But we were trapped in this frantic dynamic thinking we had found the holy grail. Me as well believed everything and didn't question everything. Otherwise I would not be here but at home with my family.« Nasrallah tried another approach. »Your belief wasn't strong enough if some Kufar could make you question all that we know to be true. The desire for the west. You yourself chose the name Abu Lot, because the west is rotten and I tested with immorality.« Abu Lot didn't want to hear the propaganda. »Oh please stop it. What we do with the sex slaves, is that moral? He made a hand gesture cutting off the caliph. »I don't want to hear a word. And of course everybody who wants to get out, is weak and has failed. Very effective strategy, because the young men don't want to be regarded as weak. So it creates a lot of pressure for every single one, especially in a herd of sheep repeating everything without thinking. You coudn't ever have a discussion about an issue because there was only the position of the emir and if you didn't follow that, they called you a Kufar. I had doubts and critic many times, But I never said something because I didn't dare to be the one criticizing the emir.« He sniffed contemptuously. »Maybe you're right and there are points to improve. Then help us get stronger.« Abu Lot cut him off in a quiet voice now. »I don't have desire for the west. I have desire for revenge. Revenge for having baited us like dogs and turned us into pit bulls.« He stood up. »I now speak to the one and only god, who is no god of hate and killing. I deeply regret having caused a lot of suffering with my weapon. Like a wild animal. But blinded human with a Kalashnikov is worse. We destroyed families, killed men and abused women and children. In the name of god. This madness has to stop. Allah Akbar!« In this moment he pulled the trigger of his belt. The last thing he heard was a click.

Jake was filling out the knowledge test. The fellow participants sat like college students on their wooden chairs with
folding table focused on the questionnaires. There was no
attandence. At least none present in the room. There was a
360 degree camera located in the center of the ceiling, but
the participants didn't know that. His special friend Malcom
sat two rows ahead of him and pinned the pencil in his
fingers non-chalantly. Involunarily Jake shook his head.
Fortunately their encounter on the first day was not part of
the program. Otherwise he probably wouldn't be here. Adriana had scolded him for his unprofessional behavior. He
had to restrain himself for the team and for Yusuf.

The test was a mix of IQ-test and crossword puzzle. »What is
the name of the dog of the American president?«, was one
question Jake pondered over. He had heard the name many
times, but when you needed such irrelevant knowledge it
wasn't there. Damn.

Slowly a prickling sensation crept up his stomach. And he
knew what it was. The participants were given a considera-
ble dosis of LSD before the test. Under these exacerbated
circumstances the ability to concentrate was tested. That
was 20 minutes ago. And it was kicking in slowly. He had
never taken it before. But he had heard from friends that
your senses was sharpened on a trip. By now he didn't feel
any extension of the synthetic sense or memory spectrum.
Nonetheless he was stimulated and something was brewing
in his neuro-cerebral anterior lobe. He fought back, didn't

want to give in to the drug. The racing of the heart? Normal tension in a test situation. »Dog name was Snoopy«, without fully remembering the question. »What is the smallest continent of the earth?« He reclined thinking.

He wondered if there were participants who had prior experience with LSD. He bet that Malcom had tried it before. He looked for his colleague, but he wasn't at his seat. Instead he was wandering around with the questionnaire copying answers from other participants. Their eyes met and Malcom waved at him and winked ironically. Jake shook his head demonstratively.

But Malcom wasn't finished clowning. He imitated the movement of a figure skater doing a triple tulip shooting the puck with a slap shot. Jake couldn't hold back a laugh. He was a funny guy, this Malcom. But back to the Question Europe or Antarctic?« His thoughts faded away again. »Why they call it old Europe? Sure, the Roman Colosseum and the greek Metropolis were old. But the glaciers in the Antarctic were far older. He didn't know about the latest Iglu models, but he committed himself: The Antarctic was the oldest planet of the world!« What were the others doing?

One participant called Vinnie had eyes big like plates and the look of a zombie. He stared out the window as if I was being followed by vultures. Jake shook his head quizzically. »He probably failed the test already.« There were people with no self control. Who just couldn't handle it. But he had a strong character and for that reason the drug didn't affect him that much. Malcom appeared in front of him. »What does a pasta in a bank?« Malcom shrugged his shoulders expecting a bad joke. »Opening a joint account!« He burst into laugh. The thick dreadlocks seemed even funnier viewed up close. Almost like thick Macceronis - al nero di seppia. He made a mental note to focus on such details in the future.

He was hot and got up. He felt unusually light. »What is actually feeling? Feelings are nothing but perceptions of the body or thoughts. They translate the respective body or life conditions into the language of the mind. Feelings are sensors for the inner state. He reached the conclusion: His inner state was just fine. He should work out again. He was a good sportsman, until puberty. But then he broke his arm and unfortunately never reached his old level. He took the questionnaire to answer the next question. Fascinated he gazed at the letters blurring before his eyes. »Language is something unique. The words of a language name things, sentences connect the words. Other animals are not able to do that. Monkeys communicate with noises and mimic. That was the origin of language! He realized.

He went to the window. There was the van where Adriana and her friends were sitting. He waved at Hola, gran abrazo!« He thought of other Italian words. »Grande Cazzo.« He waved again. Strudding back to his table he felt exhilarated. He spread his arms. »If man was as streamlined as a bird, and could run as fast - No you would need longer wings.« He reasoned. He sensed a motion behind him. Malcom did breakdance on the floor. He became dizzy from watching him and sat down in the lotus position. »Most people waste their lives thinking about the future, but the only thing that counts is the present moment. In the decisions we make in this moment, they are based on either love or fear. Many people walk the path of fear, who hide under the disguise of practicability. What we really want seems unbelievably distant and unreachable and that's why we don't dare to ask the universe for it.« He shook his head. »From now on I will spend more time with my friends. Going to the movies or to the lake. Well, maybe not not the movies right now.« He breathed in and grinned. »What a beautiful day.« He had a dry throat. »A beer would be nice.«

Adriana, Ortega and Chad sat in the van opposite of the university facility shaking their heads in disbelief. They could barely believe their eyes. There was Jake at the window waving at them and grinning like the joker. He seemed to yell Adriana's name followed by an obscene gesture. Then he danced back into the room. Ortega took off his headphones. »I think we can end this farce. We won't learn anything important today.« He told Chad to come with him. »Let's use the opportunity to see where the professor is living. And Adriana. You stay here and give our undercover agent a ride home.« He laughed again. Adriana blushed. After all she had prepped Jake and now he was being a complete disaster.

121

The house of the professor was in a residential area with big villas about 20 minutes from the psychiatric facilities. Chad had received the address via radio by a colleague in the Miami department. Woody was the only other person privy to the operation. »The professor has a wife and two children. So don't be seen«, he warned them. It was late afternoon when the rented Mitsubishi stopped in front of the house. They waited. From inside they could not discern any movement. »I go in.« Ortega got out of the car and rang the bell. If somebody opened he had to improvise. But the door remained shut. The house was empty.

He inspected the windows at the first floor but they were also closed. He stepped into the back yard. And instantly noticed that the balcony door was tilted. The balcony was at the height of about 2.80m consisting of wooden beams. Between them was room for two fingers. He wiped his hands on his pants looking up at the first beam. As a youth he had played basketball and was able to dunk the ball. So this should be easy. He crouched, thrusting his arms back, pressed the heels into the ground and released. But he wasn't even close. Chad who was standing at the corner couldn't hold back a smile. »That's what you call overestimating your abilities.« He approached his friend and offered him a hand. Ortega scratched his head. Apparently he became old. He stepped on his friend's shoulder and reached the balcony. He opened the tilted door and stepped into the room. He didn't know exactly what he was looking for, but this was definitely not the right room. It was the nursery. He stepped on the stairs and peered down. There were the living room, kitchen and bathroom. He was looking for the study, that had to be upstairs. And he found it in a spacious room in the attic. He went behind the big wooden desk crammed with newspaper articles. The first article he saw, was a coverage about the Black Jack killer. Nothing unusual these days. He took another article. It was a statistic of immigration of muslim countries in the US. The professor seemed to be quite interested in that topic. But nothing out of the order. He kept looking. There were some books on the shelves. He took the one book protruding and read the title: »They called themselves the KKK.« He put it back and took the next book that read: ‚the lynching'. He put it back and found out that most of the books were about the Clan. Could it be that the professor was a member of the KKK? It was just a suspicion. He needed to find more. He went back to the desk. Suddenly his phone vibrated. He answered. It was Chad: »You had to get out, the professor has returned.«

He needed some more time. With quick hands he rummaged through the shelves. He found a Quoran and opened it. He heard noises, The professor came up the stairs. There were notes in the Holy book and he quickly scanned the first note. »Sure 2, Vers 216: Fighting has been enjoined upon you while it is hateful to you. But perhaps you hate a thing and it is good for you; and perhaps you love a thing and it is bad for you. And Allah Knows, while you know not.« He wanted to check out another note. » Sure 8, Vers 12: I will cast terror into the hearts of those who disbelieve. Therefore strike off their heads and strike off every fingertip of them." He put it back and exited the room through the window.

They sat in the main room of the little house with only one candle spending light. Koletzki and Elena were on the couch cuddling and talking. Chris was emotionally agitated. He thought about his friend who had finally sacrificed his life for the good. That moved him. Like all the young men who had set out to find a meaning in life the only thing they found was a quick death. That made him angry. He was re-minded of the rat catcher of Hameln luring away the child-ren. He knew from his personal experience how receptive and naive a young man could be if in a difficult life situation. In a way he even had compassion for these lost souls. On the other hand they were the ones they were hiding from. He looked at Paulsen stoically waiting for the rescue to arrive. He noticed his companion's agitation and tried to soothe him. »Abu Lot proofed at the end that he has a good heart. And that he was mislead by maybe even good intentions.« He padded him on the. Shoulder. Koletzki having overheard their conversation joined in. »Like all the fighters that are convinced to do good while in reality spreading fear and ter-ror. But eventually the memory of love could bring him back on the right path. And it takes a lot of courage to go against your brothers.« Elena was hugging him from behind. »Yes it's true. It is the power of love that could brake the spell and bring them back to their senses.« She kissed Koletzki gently on his forehead.

In this moment a faint crackle could be heard from outside. Originating rotors of a helicopter cutting through the air. They ran out on the veranda in the backyard. Despite of the cold Chris suddenly had wet hands. In anticipation of the rescue he put his hands around Paulsen's shoulder. But when Paulsen looked at him irritated he took away his hand. In the pitch black night they couldn't recognize anything. They just heard the crackle become louder. »They switched off the lights.«, Paulsen mumbled. »Let's pray, it will be alright.« They stood in the cold gazing at the black night sky. Suddenly glaring lights appeared coming from the ground to the sky making a noise like a new years rocket. »Oh damn, These are FLAGS.« Paulsen exclaimed appalled. »They hit the heli...« Before he finished his sentence one of the flashes had hit an invisible target in the sky. There was an explosion and a big ball of fire tumbled to the ground burying their hope for rescue. Shocked and speechless they gazed in the direction of the crash site about 7 miles from them. That was their fate sealed now? For some moments nobody said a word. Only the gunshots of the fighters woke them up from their stupor. Paulsen dialed his number again. »Hallo, Yes we saw it with our own eyes. What there will be no other rescue team?« He hang up and looked to his friends. »We are no on our own.« With frustrated faces they went back into the house.

»Do you really think, he might be a member of the KKK?« Adriana asked surprised, after Ortega had told her about his findings. They were sitting in the hotel room drinking a glass of wine, while Chad kept observing the professor. »I don't know for sure, but I have a gut feeling that he is a staunch racist.« He looked at Adriana's tight sports pants as she re-filled his glass. »Well, we will find out, if he has dirt under his carpet.« They clinked glass and and Adriana sat close to him on the sofa. »How is Jake?« Ortega wanted to know. Adriana turned her eyes and laughed. »He was hitting on me the whole ride back. But in a nice way. I gave him a hug and he was satisfied.« Ortega laughed and kept gazing at Adria-na. »The program started with a bang. But if anything, they just look for the right candidates for the actual program.« Adriana stretched her back. »We should focus on the profes-sor.« She said casually leaning in on Ortega and putting her head on his chest. He gently stroked her hair out of the way and massaged her neck and throat applying controlled pres-sure with his thumb along the veins. »That is good. I like that.« Adriana moaned. »I want you.« Ortega came close and kissed her neck making Adriana moan more. He turned her head towards him and stroked her lips without saying anything. She sucked at his finger looking him deep in the eyes. He grabbed her gently around the neck and kissed her intimately. He had waited so long for that first kiss. At first tentative then more intense. »Mi amor«, she moaned. Ortega helped her out of her sports bra and grabbed her tight breasts. He stroked her hard buds and sucked on them. They smelled like honey and he couldn't get enough. »Quiero was«, Ortega whispered, taking off his shirt. Adriana touched his pants where a big bulge was forming. She looked him in the eyes and slowly opened the zipper. With every touch grew the passion and they soon played Allegro.

Exhausted and satisfied they lay in bed hugging. She had the feeling that her husband had given her the blessing of moving on with her life. He wanted her to be happy. And Ortega made her happy. »Que maravilloso«, she whispered in his ear. »I told you I am Leon the professional.« Ortega replied giving her another passionate kiss.

»Hallo?« Jed Collins was steering his car, when he answered an unknown number. As this was a secure line, it had to be from Iraq. »Asalamalaikum, Mr. Collins. This is Abu Qatada. Unfortunately I have bad news.« He made a long pause as if to gather himself. Then he said. »Nasrallah is dead.« Again a pause. Cracking in the line. The stock palpable. »Who?« Jed Collins asked after a while. »The brother Abu Lot turned against us.« Jed Collins stopped at the parking lane and listened to Abu Masala. »Probably these German agents turned him against us.« Jed Collins punched against the dash-board. »Where are they?« »Well, there was an explosion in the castle the were held. But we don't know for sure if they died in it or if it was a mere distraction.« Paulsen shook his head vehemently. »No, They are alive and escaping. We have to find them and punish them.« »Yes Sir, Thank you Sir, you know we have lost two of our highest men, that is why we are in disarray now. But I do what I can to organize the search.« »You get all the help you need. We stay in con-tact.« Before Jed Collins hung up he said. »And Abu Masala, you are now the second man in the Islamic State, you know that. Gain the trust if your brothers by finding and punis-hing the enemies. We talk later. Get to work.« After he hung up he la his forehead on the steering wheel and closed his eyes. He knew Nasrallah for a long time, long before the Is-lamic State. Even if he had his own mins, they had always treated each other with respect. He regarded him as a friend. He was surprised how real the pain felt. Nobody had seen the caliph or emir, because he didn't really exist. It was an invention, like Osama bin Laden. In reality Nasrallah was the first man. That was why it was such a big blow for them. He has been an intelligent and capable leader. It would be difficult to replace him equally. Until the Abu Masala would have a try, but he didn't hold him in high regard. He took a sip of his little whiskey bottle that was under his armrest. They needed to catch the Germans. He would have to deal with it himself.

Chapter 19

»Hurry. It won't take long until they'll find us.« Chris was the first to regain his poise. »You said, you have worked on a plan to escape the Islamic State before you were captured, weren't you.« He addressed the couple. »What was it?« Koletzki nodded restoring new hope. »Follow me, I show you something.« He lead them to his little shack and opened the door. In the flashlights emerged a vehicle with two seats and a little loading area. »I worked months to make it run again«, Koletzki said proudly. Chris wiped his eyes in disbelief. It looked like something you see in the 3rd world at the roadside with a break down. »And it has four wheels or two?« Koletzki ignored Chris' comment. It is inconspicuous. That is the only chance to slip under the radar. Now more than ever. « Paulsen inspected the loading area. »There is room for two persons. And the tank is full«, Koletzki explained. »But before we can go, we have to change clothes.« He changed a look with Elena. They went back into the room where Elena pulled out a box and emptied it on the table. There were a mirror, make up, false lashes etc. »We are running for our lives and you want to put on make-up?« Chris grumbled indignantly. »Chill man!« Elena smirked and looked Chris into his eyes so that he involuntarily quivered. »We work on a disguise here. So if you would give us some room please. We have to change. In the meantime you can study the map and find out an exit route.« She handed the map to Paulsen. The withdrew in the kitchen and let the hosts dress up. The route was already marked with a red line. The line meandered towards the iraqi-iranian border, where a name was underlined in bold. Chris and Paulsen changed a meaningful look. »That's a piece of cake.«

After about 40 minutes Elena and Koletzki called their friends who were nervously waiting for them. They entered the living room and wer instantly flabbergasted how they had transformed into old people. A hunchbacked old man with a long white beard, wrinkled face and hanging tear sacs and and a wobbly dame in a burka were standing in front of them shaky and mutually supporting themselves. »What you say now? Am I a good make-up artist?« Elena asked provocatively. Chris nodded his head appreciatively. »My compliment, I would never recognize you.« He Scrutinised the wrinkles in Koletzkis face. »You look like a giant turtle. Did you apply make up or just wash it off?« She slapped him gently on the shoulder and laughed.

It was three o'clock in the morning and they were ready to head out. But Paulsen hesitated. »We have to decide if we want to leave now or at dawn. Because I'm sure that every car will be checked now. But it's also too risky to stay here till morning.« They thought about the options for a minute. But neither seemed to appealing. Suddenly Elena yelled. »I have an idea! What if we go to that place in the woods where we used to swim? We could stay there till dawn and then get going.« Koletzki gave her a kiss. »That's a good idea. It's a safe place. Now let's go.« They cushioned the loading area with blankets and covered them with a tarp. Upon instructions of Paulsen they put some boxes underneath so that it had the form of something bulky. Then they got in and drove to said place in the woods.

After just a few minutes of a bumpy ride they turned into a track that became narrower and narrower until the undergrowth was so tight that they couldn't go any further by car. The mere thought of lying on the loading area for many hours on these bumpy roads gave Chris back pain already. Despite of the blankets he was cold and he realized not having eaten since breakfast. As they had found nothing edible in the house the only thing to fill their stomaches was hot tea from a thermos bottle. Paulsen looked at his shaking friend. »Sunrise will be in about 4 hours. Let's try to get soome sleep. Tomorrow will be an exhausting day.« Chris nodded gloomily. »Yes indneed.« Touching the cold barrel of the Kalashnikov.

.

Chapter 20

Abu Masala had assembled his men for an emergency mee-ting, The news of the death of Nasrallah had paralyzed them. But now it was time for action. He was now in charge of the-se men and he didn't want to disappoint the emir. One of his men put him up to date. »Abu Hattab's car was found in front of a house on the outskirts. But the house was empty.« »Damn it. This yesidi slave had helped them.« Abu Masala exclaimed. »We should have never let her run around like a freely. I always told Nasrallah.« He massaged his temples. »Ok, we have to cut off all possible escape routes and check every car, no matter what. Inform the local police about it and give them a detailed description. We can't do more mi-stakes now, brother.« »Allahu Akbar.« The brother said and left.

Abu Malst wanted to get up when he suddenly felt dizzy. »Abu Lot, how could you?« He rubbed his injured knees. The had grown up together and gone to school together.« They had fought injustices wherever they saw them and al-ways made an effort to make a difference. That was why they came here to do Dschihad. He had always envied his friend for his position and his ability to make friends easily. But now that he was gone, he missed him. He was the only per-son he had really trusted. The only person he had told about his aching knees. The only person he told he had ordered shampoo and lotion from fighters. And the only person he could talk about how he missed his mother. He couldn't think of her without becoming overwhelmed by deep sadness. In these rare moments he was Christian again. The good-natured obstinate child. She had given up trying to persuade him to come back home. Even if it was her only wish to see her son again. She even would have taken the burden to come to Syria for that. But he didn't want that. AT the end of every skype call he urged him to promise that he used his social and creative skills rather than murdering people. But also there she got an evading response. Abu Lot and his mother were the only persons that reminded him of the old Christian. But Abu Lot was dead and his mother far away. He had to be strong for the Islamic State was depending on him more than ever.

The next morning Chris was woken by a distant splattering noise. He turned around and noticed that Paulsen was not there. He crept out of the tarp and noticed that the others were also not there. The sun was up and he let the sun rays warm his face for a moment. His limbs were stiff and he felt like an old man.

After the endeavors of the passed day he had fallen into a deep, dreamless slumber. The stress started to be felt more and more. He listened to where the splattering was coming from. He went through the undergrowth and after a few yards he saw Paulsen taking a bath in the creek. »Good morning, night cap.« He seemed to be in a good mood. With time he had learnt to read Paulsen better. And he knew, the situation was serious enough so the best thing to do was to not take it seriously. »Well, I need my 10 hours of beauty sleep. Didn't I tell you that at the job interview?« Paulsen chuckled. »Well, I could use a cozy bath.« He took off his shoes and touched the water with his toes. »Ahh it's frigging' cold.« »Come on, Sissy. It wakes up your senses and we have to be alert all the time. So jump in. If an old man can do it, you can do it as well.« Chris reluctantly took off his clothes and glided into the water with a painful face. His heart pumped and he did some fast swimming strokes. »This is good. I should do this more often.« He yelled

»What's the noise about?« Koletzki yelled, standing by the shore with Elena in their fancy dress. »Morning exercise, and what about you, old people?« Chris laughed squirting water on Koletzki. »I did my morning toilet s little up the stream.« He joked. » Ah yup, I just finished my exercise.« Chris said and nude as he was climbed out of the creek. »Elena, look away. This is something you don't want to see.« He winked at her. »I'll be at the car darling. And Chris, you should really learn how to impress women.«

When they gathered at the car, they had a last talk. As on the loading area you couldn't hear what was said in the car, they agreed on knock signs. »One knock means: attention! Knocking twice means: Attack!« Paulsen explained the commandos. They hugged and wished themselves good luck. »Let's go home!« Chris shouted before he disappeared under the tarp.

The roads were barely frequented in this rural area. At a strong pace - as fast as the busy roads permitted - they advanced towards the highway to Erbil. There would be heavy traffic allowing them to submerge. But they had to be alert in every moment.

After an hour Chris and Paulsen heard a knock. They had arrived at the last checkpoint before the Erbil highway. Three police cars blocked the road and stopped every car heading to Erbil. Koletzki checked his face in the mirror before winding down the window and slowly approaching the police men. One of them was barely 16 years old. »What is your destination, old man?« He asked with a voice of authority. »We want to go to Erbil. Our son was injured in battle and we want to visit him in hospital.« Koletzki answered in impeccable Arabic. The young man looked inside the window watching Elena fidgeting with her prayer bead and staring on the ground. »Are you only two people? What's in the back?« »Yes, only us. We have some blankets and clothes for our dear son, Allay may bless him.« Koletzki answered reverently.

With the Kalashnikov cocked Paulsen and Chris listened to the conversation - ready for mayhem any moment. The boy pondered, than went to the loading area. »Let me just peak inside, and then you can go.«

Chris felt his presence in front of the tarp. He could hear him breathing in the cold air and exhaling through the mouth. Another man approached and said something in Arabic. Instantly the boy began tampering with the tarp. Chris' heart was pumping, when the tarp came off. The blankets and boxes were arranged so that you couldn't see the bodies at first sight. They would have the surprise effect on their side. His finger on the trigger trembled and beads of sweat were dripping down his forehead. He looked at Paulsen, who slowly shook his head. His face was dead serious and petrified. Chris had never seen him - or anyone - focused like this. Paulsen' jaw muscles were tight and he was ready for action like a shark before the deadly attack. The boy grabbed the blanket and was about to lift the upper layer, while talking to his colleague who was standing by. Above the car noises and the buzzing voices Chris heard the blanket fall to the ground. Then the second. The boy reached for the last layer. Chris changed a look with Paulson who nodded his head. He saw the blanket being lifted up and could see the blue sky above. As soon as the face appeared the would wreak havoc. What a nice blue sky!«

Suddenly they heard shouting voices in the background. The boy let go of the blanket and hurried over to his colleagues. After 5 minutes he came back to Koletzki. In the meantime a queue of cars had piled up. »You said you wanted to go visit your son?« Koletzki nodded. »Abdullah, he is your age.« The

136

boy gazed at them and at the cars behind him. »Ok have a good journey.«

Koletzki started his car and drove off. They rode for 5 minutes in silence then he honked to let their friends in the back know that they were in safety for now. Chris and Paulsen let go of the Kalashnikovs and hugged each other. Chris wiped the sweat with his sleeves. It would take some more minutes until his heart slowly stopped racing and the tension in his muscles dissolved.

Peep, peep, peep. Ortega woke up alarmed. He had slept about two hours with Adriana in his arms when Chad tore them out of his dreams. »He's leaving the house now. Let's go«, he informed Ortega. Adriana was awake instantly. They dressed hastily and ran to the van. Ortega steered the car with Chad on the phone directing him. »He's driving in the city center. So he's passing you by.« They stopped at the main road and waited. Meanwhile Ortega looked at Adriana skeptically who was putting make up on in her sexy black dress and stilettos. »Do you have a date? Or some other plans?« Adriana shrugged and smiled at him. »I have a gut feeling that the professor likes sexy women. I might have an opportunity to use my charm on him.« She sprayed some perfume on her neck. »You jealous, Latino?« She asked ironically. Ortega shook his head. »Zzz you are a piece of work.« She came close and kissed him on his lips. »Don't worry, I'm a good student.« »And I am a strict teacher.« He teased her.

»Hello, guys? I'm still on the phone. I didn't want to disturb your private moment, but the professor is passing you by.« Chad interrupted. »It's the blue BMW.« Ortega started the engine and chased after the BMW in a subtle distance. After quarter of an hour the BMW turned into a side street looking for a parking space. The area was packed with fancy bars and hotels. They rode around the block and found a parking space opposite the bar the professor had entered. »The professor is mine.« She said self-assured. She fumbled with some bag that contained a whit powder. Ortega frowned at her. »What is this?« Adriana showed it to him. »That is Scopolamine aka Burundanga. My brother gave it to me.« She said smiling. »All you need to do is bring it into contact with the person and he the person will lose all his resistance and will. They basically do everything you want them to do. They call it devil's breath.« Ortega had seen a lot of things as police officer but that was new to him. »What is your brother doing again. I might pay him a visit some time.« He winked at Adriana. In this moment Chad entered the van and glanced at Adriana. »Que guapa, now do what you do best and earn daddy some money.« She punched him in the stomache. »Sure, Daddy.« Ortega handed her a small bug in the form of a chewing gum. »Take this and place it near the professor, so we can hear what he's talking - if he's talking.«

Adriana entered the bar. She noticed at first glance that it was a chic place and she was glad to have chosen her elegant dress. She looked around and saw the professor sitting alone at a table on the side. She passed the bar in a fast pace. But when she was next to the professor she snapped on her high stilettos and had to hold on to the back of his chair to not fall down. The professor jumped up and lent her a hand. »Young lady, are you ok?« »Yes, thank you Sir, these shoes are terrible. I'm so sorry.« She thanked him with a seductive look and continued on to the bar.

In the car Ortega couldn't help but smiling at Chad. »She is gooood.« The bug was in place. He turned the speakers up. Chad nodded in agreement. »She's a good match for you.« Ortega looked at him but there was no ironic undertone.

In this moment an Audi drove in front of the bar and parked on the sidewalk. A man in a suit got out and hurried into the bar.

The professor got up and greeted his old friend. »Jed Collins. Nice to see you, my friend.« They cordially shook hands. The professor noticed the stressed expression in the face of his friend. »Is something wrong? You look pale.« The CIA man ordered a glass of whiskey on the rocks and then turned his attention to his friend. »There are several problems. I don't even know where to begin. First things first. We have problems with Zaidi. I was informed that he might be a problem in the trial. He starts to question the whole thing and fights against the drugs we are giving him.« The professor bit his tongue. »He should never have survived. This was a big mistake! The program is not intended for long term effects. It is more likely a suicide commando.« Jed Collins waited until the waiter put down the ordered drinks. Then he replied. »Yes that was a mistake. Our agent said he pulled the trigger, but the gun blocked. I don't know what really happened. But anyways, now we have to adjust to the new situation. During the trial we can't do anything under the public eye. That is why I'm here. We need you to get him a new memory booster. To prepare him for trial and make a fast confession.« The professor nodded his head. «I can sure try. Can you bring him to my facility?« Jed Collins nodded.

Adriana looked over her shoulder to the table, but she couldn't hear a word from the bar. She hoped Ortega had a good reception.

»He passed all the tests quite well, he was a good subject. So it will be no problem to bring him back into rythm. So rest assured, my friend.« He raised his glass and toasted to his friend. »But you said there was another issue.« Jed Collin sighed. »Yes it's becoming complicated. With the last suicide attack we might have crossed the line. They threatened to cut the budget for our islamic groups if another attack occurred on American soil.« The professor shrugged his shoulders. »We don't need another attack. We have reached our aims. The population has understood that the Islam is a vio-

140

lent and backwards religion and they don't want them here anymore.« Jed Collins looked at his glass pensively. »We need every new soldier on the front. They had major losses and need to regroup. There might also be some battle fatigue among the young men. Let's bring in some fresh elements.« The professor nodded. »No problem, that's what I'm here for.« Jed Collins emptied his glass. Abruptly he added. »Nasrallah is dead. Killed by one his most trusted fighters.« The professor was shocked. »That's not good at all. Is it?« Jed Collins shook his head. »And the agents who turned the fighter are on the run with Abu Hattab.« There was a pause. »You have to find them. The professor remembered Abu Hattab. »What was his name again, Koletzki? Yes I remember. He was the first subject we used in the territory of the Islamic State. The doctors learned the techniques quite fast. And he also defected?« »Yes he apparently fell in love with a yesidi woman and she turned him.« The professor shook his head. »Always these women.«

Chapter 21

The ride was as bumpy and hard as predicted, although Koletzki carefully tried to circumvent the holes in the street. Chris' whole body ached and the pain in the back was unbearable. Adding to that they had not eaten for more than 24 hours. Koletzki made a stop at the gas station. »How are you doing.« He whispered through the tarp, pretending to talk to someone on the phone. »We have to take a break and eat something.« Chris shot back. »How long does it take?« »About 3 hours, because we have to do some detours. But we take a break now as fast as possible.« Chris and Paulsen took a relieved breath. »Is either of you vegetarian?« Koletzki asked. »Otherwise I get burgers?« Paulsen looked at Chris laughing, but he said nothing. »Bring as much as you can carry, dumbass!«

Koletzki stopped at a restaurant and bought food to take away. Then he followed a little street along the river, they had seen from the highway, until they found a spot hidden by bushes, which they believed to be safe. As soon as the car came to a standstill he knocked on the door. Chris was the first to jump out of their torture chamber. He looked quite pale and meager in the bright sunlight, and gratefully warmed up his aching and stiff limbs. Meanwhile Elena and Koletzki unfolded the dishes at a nice and sunny spot behind the embankment. It was a feast: Burger and French fries with Coke. Chicken Wings and more french fries and chili Sauce. And for desert they had cookies and chocolate bars. Nobody said a word. It was pure blissful eatery. After they had enough, they reclined enjoying the sun. Chris would have loved to take a nap. But that was not possible. He looked at the map over Paulsen's shoulder. Now that he saw it in bright daylight he made a sober discovery. »These zig-zag lines, do they mean that there is a mountain?« »Yes«, Elena replied. »We chose the Shiphar mountains, because they are only about 3000m high.« Chris involuntarily looked at his sneakers. »Only 3000m? Are there even higher mountains?« »Yes, in Kurdistan there are mountains up to 4500m. So we are well off.« Chris whistled surprised. »I hope our car has four wheel drive.« Koletzki shook his head. »There is a mountain pass. But it is further south and way too dangerous. They shoot from both sides at people they don't know. It is safer to walk.« An awkward silence arose, until Paulsen got up. »Let's get started, we need to arrive before sunset and find a place to spend the night.

Ortega and Chad were dumbfounded. They had heard the whole conversation. »I wonder what they mean by ‚getting Zaidi back on track'«, Ortega told his friend. »That didn't sound good. They want to get rid of him as soon as the trial is over.« Chad repeated pensively.

They saw the professor saying goodbye to the man in the suit. »We follow him, but first I have to make sure Adriana is safe.«

He was about to enter the bar when the man in the suit met him at the swinging door. For a moment they looked at each other, then he moved on and saw Adriana at the bar. The professor had joined her and they were talking. Adriana noticed Ortega and indicated to him that she took care of the professor. He hesitated a moment, but then headed back to the van.

»May I invite you for a drink, young lady?« »Sure, why not?« Adriana replied charmingly. He ordered two Martini on the rocks. »My name is Robert and your name is?« »Estefania Costa Pena. Glad to meet you, Robert.« »Have we met before? You are not one of my students, are you?« He picked up the conversation. »You want to flatter me. No I'm not a student anymore.« She stroked her strand of hair out of the face. »I'm in international relations.« She smiled mysteriously. »That sounds interesting. I could have guessed.« He paused as the barkeeper handed them their drinks. »What is a beautiful woman like you doing on her own in this bar? Are you waiting for somebody?« Adriana threw back her head and laughed affectedly. »No worries, I am on my own. I wanted to have a drink with a friend of mine, but she called it off on short notice. As I was dressed already I thought, I would still get my drink.« The professor held up his glass. »Now it's your second drink and you are not alone any longer.« They clinked glasses and Adriana glanced at him while sipping on her drink. »You are professor of what? Mathematics?« He laughed and shook his head. »Philosophy?« He laughed again. »Physics?« »No my dear, now you flattering me. »I'm professor of Psychiatry.« »Wow, interesting. So you can read people's thoughts then? Is that true« She used the stereotype question. »Well, I'm not a psychic, but I understand the working of the mind. So don't lie to me.« Adriana flinched. »Are you married, professor?« She asked in her high pitched voice. The professor's hand twitched and he tries to conceal his wedding ring. When he realized that she had seen the ring, he explained. »Seperated, not divorced yet. But only for tax reasons.« »Ah I see.« She looked lasciviously at his lips. Then she blinked. »Would you attend my drink for a moment? I go to refresh myself.« She got up and went to the toilet. When she noticed that the professor was facing the bar, she passed his former seat and stripped the bug from the chair. On the toilet she looked into the mirror and touched the package of Burundanga. It encouraged her.

»Dear Professor Robert.« She greeted him, when she came back. »My sweet Estefania.« He replied taking her hand chivalrously. »Do you want anything else to drink?« She shook her head. »No thank you, professor.« »Would like to go to another place?« He stroked her hand. »I would love to, professor.« She whispered. He paid and they walked out of the

145

bar. »The bar belongs to a hotel, where I happen to have a room.« He offered his arm to Adriana and she grabbed it.

The receptionist seemed to know the professor and greeted him friendly passing him the card for the room. When they were in the elevator the professor wanted to slip his hand under Adriana's dress. But she slapped his hand playfully. »Professor, please! Be patient, till we are in the room.« He hastily opened the door and threw himself on the sofa waiting for her. Adriana noted the fierce look in his eyes. She excused herself for a moment to go to the bath again. She nervously nestled in her bag taking some Burundanga into her hand hiding it in her fist. Slowly she approached the professor and sat on his lap facing him. »My price is 2000,- Dollar for 2 hours. Is that fine for you?« She was stroking his thigh with her right hand. »That's not a problem, my dear. Now come to daddy.« She opened her lips and came closer to his mouth. He closed his eyes in wild anticipation. Shortly before their lips met, she opened her left fist and blew the Devil's breath into his mouth. »Or is that too much for one Bungabunga.«

Chapter 22

After two more hours of driving the mountains emerged in front of them. It was late afternoon and the sun dyed the mountains in a lush green. Soon the road meandered anxiously through the mighty mountain massif, towards the district Soran. Here they wanted to spend the night and rest before the crossing the next day. The closer they came to Soran the more black flacks emerged spreading a spooky atmosphere in this colorful landscape. The district was in tight grip of the Islamic State. »Wheras the majority of people in Mosul was Sunni, here the Majority was Kurdish. The Kurds are very proud people. It was a fierce battle for this strategically important district. A lot of Kurdish fought the enemy 'til the end. It was ugly.« Elene got goosebumps. »I know the wider area. It is not far from the village I come from. They overran us, we had no chance. There was no help from neither the Syrian government, nor the Kurds, nor anyone else.« Her voice was shaking.

They had climbed up to a height of 1000m and the sun started to set. On a mountain base not far away they detected a little city. It was surreal. It looked like a city in the clouds, painted orange by the sun. They drove inside the city without being checked and parked the car in a little side street at a dead end. Koletzki looked around for passengers but when he couldn't see any, he gave the sign for Chris and

Paulsen to get out of the car. With pale and wretched faces they peeled themselves out of the loading area, like snails that were being stepped on more than once. A pitiful sight. »I'm feeling bad as well«, Paulsen whispered. »But don't let it show. We don't want to cause any suspicions.« Chris stretched his back one more time and nodded. The walked to the square on top of the plateau that was bustling with little shops and people. »This view should be a little renumeration for your hardships.« Koletzki presented them the stunning backdrop. »That is... are we in heaven?« Chris asked. »No, we are still in the Islamic State:« Paulsen rebuked him indicating at the black flags hanging from the parapets of the city wall. Chris bought a freshly pressed pomgranade juice and instantly felt his zest for life returning. »Now I know why they call Kurdistan the Switzerland of the middle east«, he joked and they laughed. Except for Paulsen who pensively gazed at the snowcapped glaciers bordering Iran.

»Abu Masala? Collins speaking. What's the situation on the ground?« Collins asked riding on a highway in direction of the rocky mountains appearing in the shimmering light of the full moon like evil spirits. »Asalamalaikum. Ja ne Mr. Collins. I'm afraid we still haven't found them. The seem to have disappeared from the surface. They must have slipped through one of the checkpoints around Mosul.« Collins scratched his head. »The nearest border is the iranian-kurdish border, right?« »Yes Sir, but it is a vast area. We might need support.« »Alright, I am on the way. I will send over air support. We stay in contact.« He reached a gate, where he had to identify himself and continued on to the main road of Fort Carson.

»Professor, I want you to show me the program, where you treated Zaidi«, Adriana ordered. She looked at the professor, yet he remained silent. The drug had turned the professor into a zombie, with no own will. Her gut feeling told her, he had something to do with Zaidi. »Show me the final phase of the program!« She tried again. »Where do we have to go?« Finally the professor opened his mouth. »To my psychiatry, the Devereux treatment center«, he murmured in a robotic voice. She lead him to hius car and sat him on the passenger seat. The professor had turned into a faithful dog, complying her orders. Adriana had to look up the directions first before she headed to Westminster, which was quite a distance from the hotel. After one hour riding through the moonlit night, they finally reached the facility. She parked the car on the parking lot that was almost entirely empty. »Pull out your identification card« , she instructed the professor. He grabbed it from under the arm rest and they left the car. She led him to the night guard and the professor presented his identification. »Good night, Professor Fitzek«, The security man greeted him. »You are working late?« He looked at Adriana curiously. »You have a good-looking company.« The professor didn't even move his lips and stared straight ahead. Adriana answered instead. »I'm his student, and He wants to show me an experimental arrangement.« She smiled naively and gave the professor a slap on the shoulder. »That is so nice of you. Now *let's go*!«, she added in her commanding tone. The security man looked puzzled after the odd couple walking towards the elevator. Then he shook his head and kept on reading his magazine.

The lighting in the reception hall was scarce and produced a spooky atmosphere. The took the elevator and the professor pressed the floor -3. The door opened and they walked into a ward that was illuminated by neon lamps. The plaster on the wall was crumbling on many spots. They walked to the end of the ward to a heavy door. »Open the door.« Adriana ordered. The professor put his thumb on the little display in front of the door and waited. After a moment the door opens automatically saying »Welcome professor Dr. Fitzek.«

They followed the red dot in the direction of Fort Carson. Chad had put a tracking device on the car of the man in the suit, while he was talking to the professor. Now they were following the signal. »I am so curious to know what he is up to know.« Chad rubbed his hands. »We're on to something big.« He added. Ortega clenched his fist. »Adriana was right from the beginning. I begin to understand why they took the case from us! We have to stop these evil people!«

They were now about a mile from the main gate of Fort Carson. From afar they saw the checkpoint where you had to identify order to pass. They looked at each other helplessly. »Damnit, it's a military facility!« Chad exclaimed. »There is now way through the main entrance. We have to find another way.« Ortega switched off the lights and drove off the main road closer to the closed off area. When they reached the fence, Ortega got out of the car. In the quiet night he could hear the crickets chirp. »I need a beer. DO you have one?« He asked. Chad looked at him in surprise. »You want to get drunk now?«

After they had bought Kurdish clothes, scarfs and trekking shoes they looked out for a kebab house for dinner. They entered a little one in a side street and sat down in the furthermost corner where they could talk undisturbed. As it was early in the evening there were only two other guests in the present. After ordering the food, Paulsen began in a low voice. »We get up early tomorrow morning. So the question is, do we stay in the car over night or risk to check into a room. »I can't stay in the car another night«, Chris stated decidedly. Koletzki frowned. »Well then we have to find a safe place. In this city Islamic State police is everywhere and random checks are conducted anywhere and anytime.« That dampened the spirits, but they knew they were wanted all over the Islamic State. That was why they had to leave as fast as possible. »But we also need a room to make preparations«, Paulsen stated. »Maybe Elena can also turn us into old men as well.« She shrugged her shoulders. »Sure. But I'm more concerned with where to find a safe place to stay? I don't think the hotels are safe here.« She waited while the waiter served the dished with the host standing behind. Elena looked at Paulsen. When they were alone again, she said. »The host is Kurdish. As most Kurds are enemies to the Islamic State we might ask him for advice on where to get shelter.« Paulsen looked at the old man behind the bar. »There is a possibility he will betray us, but I think we have to take the risk.« Paulsen decided. »Koletzky, It may be best you speak with him.« He looked around and the two guests had already left. He nodded to Koletzki who didn't hesitate. He approached the host. » *Assalamu alaikum wa rahmatullah wa barakatu.* My friend, I came here with my family and two cousins from the Mosul area. We are Shia and escaping Dawla Islamiya. We are looking for a place to stay for the night. Can you please help us? We can pay you.« The host looked at Koletzki and than at the table. »Where are you from exactly?«, he wanted to know. »The Mosul area, a village called Atabah. Look at my youngest cousin, he is in great danger.« The host seemed to waver, but after a moment said. »Sorry I'm afraid I can't help you.« It might be his accent that was putting off the host, Koletzki thught. But he wouldn't give in that easily. He leaned over the bar. . »Listen I know what you are thinking. We are not Islamic State fighters, we are German prisoners, my wife is Yesidi. We are in great danger and trying to escape to Iran.« The host looked at him despicably. »Ah you and your German friends are tourists? Now I get it. And I thought the season was over already.« He sniffed. »Now please, let me work.« Koletzki walked back to the table disappointed. »He doesn't believe me -probably thinks we're supporters of Islamic State.« Elena got up in an instant and walked straight behind the bar adressing the host. »You don't want to help us? That's fine. But then say so and don't be a coward! I'm sick of these people with no courage.« She eyed the host who looked at her surprised.« At this moment a group of guests entered the bar, so the host lowered his voice. »My dear sister, You are right, I risk my life helping you. So I need a guarantee that your German friends are not or have not been Islamic States fighters. I will not help somebody who has killed for the enemy.« As some more guests were entering now, Elena spoke in a low voice. »They are agents trying to liberate my husband, a journalist, who was captured and sentenced to death by the enemy. She lifted her gray wig a little. »We are young people. And they will kill us, like they killed almost my whole village! So please!« The host nodded slowly. »Ok ok, I believe you. You came to the right man. Now sit down. I will talk to you later.«

With a triumphant look on her face Elena returned to the table. »He will help us.« Chris almost cried out in relief but then whispered joyful. »We will make it out of here!« He would have loved to have a Cuba libre now. But that would have to wait. In the meantime the restaurant has filled. The Kurdish people wouldn't be intimidated.

Suddenly the door opened abruptly and a group of black clad men entered the restaurant. They headed for the biggest table in the midst driving away the family sitting there. The host and his water came running and helped the family find another seat. Then he took the order of the fighters. They seemed to be in festive mood and sporadically erupted in loud laughter. Paulsen looked in the shocked faces of his friends. The could only hope that the fighters wouldn't recognise them and they could sneak away. But it became worse. Two of the fighters stood up and began checking the passports of the guests. One by one. Chris' blood froze in his veins. They were so close to rescue and now this. What could they do? He looked at the host but he was busy attending the fighters. He wanted to get up and go to the toilet, but Paulsen held him back. »Don't. That's raises too much attention.« The fighters were only three tables away from them checking a couple's papers. They had to come up with something fast. Chris hands became wet. He looked at Elena who kept her eyes fixed on the host. The host approached the table handing Elena a small piece of paper, then quickly retreated back. Then he accompanied the two waiters carrying the dishes to the enemy fighter's table. Each of them balanced plates of salad, rice, vegetables and meat in their hands. But before they served the dishes the host raised his voice. »I guess, you don't pay like usually. Because you take what you want. Is that right?« One of the fighters got up and shouted. »Serve the damned dishes, Kufar. You can be lucky we let you and your people alive.« The host held back his waters. »You always take what you want. And for us the prices for food and necessities are raising every day more and more. He looked around but most people lowered their heads. But he wouldn't back down. »This time I insist that you pay me in advance.« There was dead silence and the host stared down the speaker of the group. He seemed to be caught off guard for a moment. But then he yelled. »Old man, you are playing with your life. Think about what you are doing.« He drew his gun from his holder pointing at the host. He kept looking at him unmoved. »You want to shoot an old man? Like you killed my sons and daughters? They died fighting you! I don't have nothing to lose. Now go ahead, be a brave muslim.« He looked at the guests and this time he felt the support of his people. The Islamist hesitated and looked at his friends while the host kept speaking. »Anyone of us knows at least one family member who has died or left his home.« He received approving nods by the guests. »And those who stayed, you can kill us all. But what you gain from that? Who cultivates the crop for you? Who tails your clothes? Who serves you the dishes? Who can you exploit if no-one is here?« He spread his arms like a reverend and murmur of the guests grew louder. The Islamists discussed and argued between themselves, wielding their guns. Paulsen read the situation. He got up trying to pull away the host saving him from himself. Chris and the others also got up and stepped closer. So did the rest of the guests. One of the guests shouted. »You want to shoot an old man? Because he wants to get paid for his work? Then you can shoot all of us.« The islamists almost lost their temper. »You Kufar, how dare you question our actions. Sit back down!« The situation grew tight. Other guests raised their voices against the Islamists. And some fearful guests and women and children left the restaurant. Paulsen grabbed Elena and shoved her outside as well. So did Chris with old koletzki. While emotions ran high they managed to sneak outside into the darkness. The host had saved their lives with his dangerous act. Relieved they breathed the fresh night air. Elena pulled out the piece of paper with the adress of the host's sister.

»No, I don't accept money from you«, The sister of the host said indignant, when Koletzki wanted to give her something. The small, robust woman who had presented herself as Samara, was about 50 years old and had her brunette hair at schoulder-length streaked with grey strands. »We have to hold together against a common enemy.« She showed her guests around the house. She had two rooms to give. When they had settled in, Chris and Paulsen accompanied Samara in the living room

with tea and dates. Shortly after also Koletzki and Elena appeared in the door. Samara flinched as she saw the young couple that have been old and weak a minute ago. »Don't worry Samara, we forgot to tell you that we came in disguise. Elena reached in her pocket and showed her passport. »Elena Omer«, Smart read the name and thoroughly compared the picture with Elena. »Alright, alright sit down my dear. Have some tea and some dates.« They had changed some pleasantries and Samara noticed Elena's accent. »Where are you from and what happened to your family?« Samara asked. »My family is from the city Sinschar not far away from here.« Elena explained. »Daesch was advancing towards our city and shortly before they reached our city, we packed all we could carry and set out for Silopis, a turkish city near the border. Along with thousands of other Yesidi refugees. We reached the Sindschar mountains, but there were so many people that we had to wait for 5 days in the blazing heat. We were stuck, o way ahead and no way back. We had to witness people dying from hunger and fatigue. Our group was at the foot of the mountain. And we were the first to be attacked by the islamists. We were about 100 people, family, friends, they murdered all men instantly. Women and children were massacred or raped. They chose who they could use and who was of no value to them.« She held her breath. Samara got up and gave a warm hug. »It's alright, I know how it feels. I know...« She stroked her hair until she calmed down and continued. »I was lucky and they brought me to a slave market. There this beloved man saved me and we planned our escape when they incarcerated him.« She took Koletzki's hand and pressed it against her heart. Samara refilled Elena's cup of tea. »I had a daughter that looked like you. Her name was Ronja, like the robber's daughter. I had a sense that she would be as courageous as the fictional Ronja. And I was right. When Daesh attacked she became part of the elite unit of the YPG, The women squad. They fought Daesh till the bitter end.« She halted and took a sip of her tea. »Before she was a normal student, who wanted to see the world and have a good life. But when it was time for defending her homeland, she didn't hesitate.« Samara brushed away a tear. »She was proud to be in the special unit. And she liked to make fun of Daesh. She used to mock them. »If a Daesh fighter dies in battle, he doesn't go to paradise. He goes to the kitchen and has to bake cake for eternity.« She became serious. »And she used to complained about where the Islamists get their weapons from. They are better equipped than the Kurds.« Samara got up and picked up a foto of her daughter from the commode and kissed it. »She fought brave till the very end.«

It was 2 o'clock in the morning, when Adriana and the professor were walking down the aisle of the ward, until he suddenly stopped at a door. They entered the dark room, that was illuminated by a blue flickering three big flat screens hanging from the wall. On one of them Adriana recognized charts and oscillographs with wide lashing lines. Behind the screens was a wall of glass that offered a view into a another room with two big tubes. Adriana noticed the man on night duty and he noticed them. He oddly flinched as if he was torn out of his sleep. »Professor Fitzek, I didn't know you were coming tonight«, he babbled and hastily sat upright. Surprised he gazed at Adriana, who eyed him coldly. »Tell your nightshift to *go home!*« The professor complied murmuring. »Go home.« The nightshift hesitated in the face of the strange behavior of the professor and his odd company. Adriana was forced to interfere. »My name is Alice Cooper, CIA. We don't need you anymore, thank you for your services.« She turned his back on him talking to the professor. »*Show me the files of the patient.*« The professor approached the desk taking some folders. The nightshift looked at them for another moment and then shrugged and left the room. The door closed. Time was ticking now. She opened the folder and looked it through. The first patient's name was Fashawn Lynch, 31 years, committed to a mental hospital, transferred to Devereux 2 months ago. Below was his foto and history of treatment. She opened the other file. It was Ibrahim Chengis, 24 years, student of chemistry, 2 years on parole for assault. »*Hold them*«, Adriana ordered, handing him the files She approached the desk. On the left screen she recognized the MRT's of the patients. Ibrahim was seen on the middle screen. His sight gave Adriana a shock. The young man was wearing a bonnet with innumerable wires ejecting. Like a spider web. He looked more like a trapped animal than a human. His face was cadaverous, his hair in disorder and his eyes glassy and inanimate. Adriana's heart began racing. What was going on? This was nothing she had ever seen. What was the purpose of this arrangement. But it was not hard to see, that this was amounting to torcher. She slapped the professor in the face who kept standing like an imbecile. Then she looked back at Ibrahim who seemed to move his lips along to a song. Adriana noticed the head phones in front of her lying on the desk. She put them on. It was a cacophony of noises and she turned the volume down. It was the noise she knew from a MRI scanner. She took up his file and read. »Gamma 40 Hz, isochronic sinus waves, 140 decibel. She remembered that sinus waves synchronized nerve impulses in groups of cells of the human brain. It promotes brain activity. But above the noise a voice could be heard.

»They wish you would disbelieve as they disbelieved so you would be alike. So do not take from among them allies until they emigrate for the cause of Allah . But if they turn away, then seize them and kill them wherever you find them and take not from among them any ally or helper.

Fighting has been enjoined upon you while it is hateful to you. But perhaps you hate a thing and it is good for you; and perhaps you love a thing and it is bad for you. And Allah Knows, while you know not.

Indeed, those who have believed and those who have emigrated and fought in the cause of Allah - those expect the mercy of Allah And Allah is Forgiving and Merciful.

And what is the matter with you that you fight not in the cause of Allah and for the oppressed among men, women, and children who say, «Our Lord, take us out of this city of oppressive people and appoint for us from Yourself a protector and appoint for us from Yourself a helper?«

Watching Ibrahim reiterating the words, Adriana couldn't believe her ears. She slowly began to understand, what this whole setting was about. And she knew the underlying concept. The brain needs stimulation. If there is no stimulus, the brain will create it itself. In the case of a sensoric deprivation it creates a hallugenic world, in order to get stimulus from this world. In this setting an artificial world was created by the sound nourishing the brain. They instilled hate in these feeble minds and maybe even more. She wondered for how long the men have been in the tube. Regarding the looks of Ibrahim it had to be a while.

Adriana just wanted to get the young man out of the tube, and get out of there. But she didn't know how dangerous it was for her to enter that room. She turned the page in the folder: applied drug: Synthetic Mescaline, PCP, duration of treatment: 3 weeks. From the date of the beginning she calculated he was already 10 days in the tube. She had to get him out as fast as possible. »*Stop the program and open the tubes!*«, she ordered. The professor, who had stood motionless, instantly approached the main computer pressing some buttons and making some clicks. Slowly the tubes opened up and disclosed the patients. Adriana entered the room. She passed the tube with the patient called Lynch -he gave her shudders - and moved on to Ibrahim. His state was even more wretched from up close. He stared at her with bitten lips and bewildered eyes filled with terror. His hands shook and he kept mumbling:»It is time to do Jihad. I am ready for Jihad. Adiana noticed an acrid stench. He apparently had wetted himself. She fearlessly unfastened the straps and extended her hands. »Come. Get out of there. It's over.« Ibrahim looked at her bewildered. She tried to pull him out and slowly he started to comply. But when his legs touched the ground they buckled like blades of grass. No wonder, after ten days of lying in bed. But she couldn' wait for him to recover, they had to hurry. She didn't want to test what these people were capable of if they captured her. She remembered the wheelchair at the door when entering. She unfolded it and sieved Ibrahim into it. »Now let's get out of here!«

She thought about making an emergency call, but soon found out that there was no service. She pushed Ibrahim through the door and took the folder out of the professor's hand. *»Come with me.«*

They had sat quiet for a while recovering from the journey and sunken in their own thoughts until there was a knock on the door. The host arrived. They got up end cordially greeted the man who had saved their lives a few hours ago. He now gave his friends a warm and welcoming smile. »What happened after we left? Was somebody hurt?« »No after you left, I deescalated the situation by saying that I don't want any guests to be involved or hurt and gave them their food. They will come back though and harass me again.« Koletzki felt guilty and offered him some money, but like his sister the host reclined. »No I don't take money for helping people. That is something I do from my heart.« Koletzki changed a desperate look with Elena and put the money back. The host didn't want to lose time. He pulled out a map scattering it on the table so that everybody could see. »I will show you a route, on which many brothers and sisters successfully escaped. »The border is strongly guarded and - I talked to a friend of mine - even more fighters were deployed. Apparently they are looking for 3 escaped prisoners and a yesidi woman. That should be you!« He laughed. »But why do they care so much who is escaping? The less people inside the less there is potential for riots or civil unrest? Isn't that so?« Chris wanted to know. »Yes it's true. Not for this city though. A lot of disappointed fighters sought to escape over the mountains and they try to prevent that and set an example. The fighters who got captured expect tough prison sentences or even death. But lately the numbers of escaping fighters was so high, that they had to implement this regime. That is why they only stationed the most loyal and most trusted fighters here. I know because it has become so difficult to find a mole.« He chuckled again and then painted a red thin line on the map. If you encounter someone on the way there is a 90% probability they will be Daesh. They have order to kill all of the escaping Kurds or refugees. They go by the strategy: first shoot, ask questions later. So there is no negotiating. So either hide or shoot.« He looked at them seriously. The four nodded. »Then it doesn't really matter which disguise we wear, does it?« »No, you wear camouflage! That is the only color that saves lives.« The host continued. »If you made past Daesh, don't celebrate to soon, because also on the other side there os danger. On the other side there will most likely be Kurdish soldiers. In the past there were a couple of suicide attacks targeted on them, so be careful. They might have a shaking finger on the trigger as well.« He pulled out pen and paper and began to scribble something. When he was done, he folded the paper and gave it to Paulsen. »As soon as you encounter the YPG fighters, show them this letter. It will confirm that you are friends of mine.«

Paulsen received the letter and thanked the host. »I will pick you up tomorrow at dawn. Samara will wake you up. Try to get some rest. It will be a demanding hike.« He shook hands with each of them and was about to leave when Elena held him back. »Sir, we came here with a car, that is to no use for us anymore. You might use it, to help other refugees.« The host nodded his head gratefully and Koletzki gave him the keys and the description. Then the old man left into the night.

Before going to bed, Chris stood at the terrace gazing at the starry night sky. The city was almost entirely black and behind it towered the snow giants bending down menacingly as if to say: »Don't come too close.« Paulsen appeared behind Chris and put a hand on his shoulder. »Chris, you really surprised me. At the beginning I thought, you might be more of a burden than support. But you have proven to be a hearty journalist and a good friend.« Chris was surprised to hear such words from Paulsen. »You were braver than most agents I have worked with. When we manage to return you will have an interesting story to tell and the media will be all over you. And you deserve it.« He turned Chris and looked him in his eyes earnestly. »Now we have to gather all of our strength and be focused just one more time. Then we will make it out of here.« He grabbed him by the neck amicably and pulled him close to a manly hug. Chris wondered a compliment and a hug by Paulsen? Now it really getting serious.

He had shimmering eyes and turned around facing the stars again.

»Is Islam a violent religion? After all so many people are killed in the name of Allah.« Paulsen stood next to Chris looking towards the mountains. »What we're witnessing here is terrorism. That has nothing to do with religion. It has an agenda, an objective. They attract and abuse the simple minded, those without perspective, the mentally ill people under the cover of Islam. Believe me the majority of the muslims would rather live in peace and liberty than in war or according to sharia law. Be it Sunnis or Shiites.« They saw a shooting star appear on the night sky until it ran out of gas. »You see, Islam is a religion, and as such is neither peaceful nor violent. It rather depends upon what every person brings to it. If you embrace violence, your Islam, your christianity, your buddhism will be violent.« Chris didn't seem to be convinced. »But the female circumcision, the suppression of women and such things - you don't find that in other religions?« Paulsen shook his head and sighed. »I have been to almost every muslim country on earth. In Saud Arabia they practice a complete different Islam as in Indonesia, yet both are muslim countries. Islam has more than 1,3 million adherers. And in every region it is interpreted differently. Circumcisions are a major problem in central Africa. But also it is practiced also among christians there. In Indionesia or Malaysia women are equal to men, they even have female presidents. So a lot of what we attribute to religion is in fact a regional problem.« He tapped his friend's shoulder. »I give you one advice as journalist. What you have witnessed here is the worst interpretation of Islam. But you can't take single examples and generalize them. That is the definition of bigotry, my friend. But you are better than that« Long after they went to bed, the words still rang in Chris' ears until he fell asleep.

Chapter 25

Murray and Rod had nightshift in Fort Carson. It was a balmy September night and the full moon illuminated the night sky. Rod sat in the jeep non-chalantly smoking a cigarette. Next to him was his pal Murray, a muscle man of almost 7 feet. He had taken off his army jacket and only wore a tank top. His massive arm displayed a tribal tattoo that stretched to the chest and was embellished by many patterns. Rod admired the impressive body of his friend. They had been friends for a long time and Murray knew about the little secret of his friend. He preferred men. But in the army you better kept that to yourself. »Don't ask, don't tell.« When he had started 6 years ago it was forbidden to have homosexual relationships or even to talk about related things. But on the other hand it was also forbidden to launch investigations into one's sexuality. That practice had changed. But it was still better to keep it to yourself. Except if he was with his friend Murray. »You are a beautiful man. If you were gay, we could do it right here at the outpost.« Murray was not gay but liked to receive compliments. So he played along with his friend. »I might, if you were not in a relationship.« »Oh that, we talked about it, he is fine with it.« Rob winked at him and Murray squirmed. This round went to Rob. »How many tattoos are you allowed to have? Is it still four?« Rob asked his friend. »No, you know I have more than four tattoos. They abolished that rule. Fortunately. Only face, neck and hands are not permitted.« Suddenly the radio cracked. »Zero Nine, please come. Zero None, please come.« »Zero Nine here, whassup?« »Sensors have been triggered, about a mile east of the gate. Exact position is..« There was a roar. »C1 east.« Murray took up the radio. »Roger, we check that.« They looked at each other and sighed. It was probably a rabbit or other animal that had triggered the sensor, but they had to check that. Murray put on his jacket and rode across country to the sensor. When they approached they saw from the distance that it was not an animal. In the lights of the jeep a drunk man appeared. He must have stepped over the fence. »Sir,« you illegally trespassed the property of the U.S. military base of Fort Carson. You have to immediately turn around.« He stopped when he saw that the man was swaying and obviously not listening. He stepped closer. »Sir, do you hear me? We are entitled to use force if you will not comply.« The man looked up at Murray and took a mouthful of Whiskey. »What you gonna do, asshole«, he said provocatively. »First take our weapons away and then what? If you are a man fight me with your fists!« He threw his bottle away and raised his fists. Murray changed a look with his partner. You rarely got an opportunity like this to practice your fight skills with a civilian. If the man kept asking for a pounding he would help him with that. »But he had to utter another warning first. »Sir, this is the the last warning. You are trespassing and we will use force.« The man nodded. »Come to daddy, motherfucker.« Murray pulled out his baton and was about to render a stroke, when the drunk man surprisingly skillfully dodged and wrestled him to the ground. Instantly Rob stepped closer with his taser in hand waiting for the right moment to shoot. At this moment Ortega came jumping from the side like a predator. With one punch he sent the young man in the realm of dreams. He took the taser and without wavering shot at the big Soldier lying on top of his friend. He flinched and let go of Chad. He pulled out his real gun and yelled. »Now hands up or I will shoot.« Chad pushed him to the side of the car, while Orttega aimed at him. »Now call the head quarter and tell them it was a false alarm.« He pushed the barrel against his temple. »I have been with the army. If I sense the slightest hint of a hidden warning, I shoot you! Don't test me.« Murray took up the radio still blindsided and gave the all-clear. »It was just a rabbit out here, over.« Chad handcuffed the two soldiers and tied them up at a tree. Chad took the army Jacket of Rob. »That should be my size. I always wanted to have one. Thank you Sir.« He saluted. They got into the jeep and followed the red dot again.

Chapter 26

Adriana was still under shock. She looked at the Professor and then at his former subject, Ibrahim, who was rocking forth and back in his wheelchair. It made her furious. People like the professor were - more often than not - acquitted by a white jury. She saw the injustice day by day. Little drug dealers got harsh prison sentences while the white collar criminals got parole. The professor wouldn't get off that easyily.

»*Get into the tube, Professor!*«, she demanded. »I need your thumb. Show it to me.« The professor did as ordered. Adriana put his thumb on his knee and started cutting off the finger tip with her knife. She had to use all her strength to cut through the bone, but her anger gave her energy. Besides she needed the fingerprint to get through the door. With trembling hands she wrapped the severed thumb in a paper and put it away in her bag. Than she went back and started the program with the professor inside. With satisfaction she saw the tube closing and the voice starting again. »Burn in hell! Hijo de puta!« She screamed.

She remembered Ibrahim. A thread of saliva hanging out of his mouth. He needed her help. She couldn't lose her poise now. »Calmate Adriana, calmate.« She told herself taking a deep breath. She hastily put the folder in and her bag in Ibrahim's lap and pushed him out the door. When she stepped on the floor, she instantly realized that her stilettos would be a handicap, so she took them off. Barefooted she pushed the Ibrahim to the door and tried to use the severed finger tip. But it was too bloody for the scanner. Appalled she cleaned it with a napkin and tried it again. At the third try the scanner accepted the finger and the door clicked open. Disgusted she threw away the finger tip and carefully peeked into the hallway. To her right was the elevator. She was about to push the wheelchair in that direction when suddenly she heard rapid steps by at least more than two men coming from the elevator. They were looking for her. Her heartbeat was 180 now. She had to find cover but where? The next corner to her left was about 15 meter from her. Too far. She opened the nearest door and slipped inside with Ibrahim, without knowing who or what would be inside. When the door went shut she had to go down on her knees. She was about to black out, and that literally, because the room was pitch black. »Did you see the ball of fire?« A voice asked and Adriana almost would have screamed out. The voice was right next to her. »Hallo?« She switched on the flashlight on her phone and illuminated the person. It was a small middle aged woman holding a blanket in her hands. »Did you see the fire ball?«, the woman repeated. Adriana now illuminated the whole room and witnessed that there were several beds. She turned to the woman. »What's your name?« With her heart still thumping, she looked at the woman closer. She ha to be around 40 years old, but already had plenty of grey hair. Her eyes were wide open and she had big black and dilated pupils as if they had given her Bella Donna. »My name is Caro.« She answerd. »What are they doing with you here Caro?« The crazy looking woman shrugged her shoulders. »They help us with our problems. And they help us sleep. And sometimes they shoot fireballs at us, which is no fun.« Her glassy eyes gave Adriana shudders. But she seemed to be trustworthy. »We are followed by evil men. Can you help us?« » I don't know if I can«, Caro answered in her monotone voice. »Are there cameras in this room?« »Yes, Marcus said there are cameras. But he also said, the nurses were always asleep at night.« »Ok, good. As I told you, we are followed by these men and I need your help.« »No fireballs?« »No I promise, no fireballs.« She told Caro what she had to do and gave her a hug. Then Caro opened the door and stepped out on the floor. She turned around and smiled. »No fireball.« Then she ran as fast as she could.

Adriana turned her attention to Ibrahim, who seemed to be asleep. She took a new handkerchief and cleaned his mouth. »Everything will be alright. I'll bring you back to your family. They miss you.« She put her hand on his shoulder and stroked it.

Chapter 27

It was 6 o'clock in the morning, when Samara entered their room and tore Chris out of his dreams. As soon as he was awake he wanted to know how the weather was. No clouds. Perfect conditions for a hike.« Samara calmed him. She had brought a sack with clothing in camouflage. They put on some fitting garments. Chris thought how lucky they were to have found these good people who were so well organized. When he was fully dressed and looked like John J. Rambo, he met his friends at the richly set breakfast table. »Good morning everybody.« The host appeared in the door with a hearty smile. »The weather report foresaw a sunny day. Let's hope he is right for once.« H laughed. Chris wondered how many people he and his sister had helped to escape from the Islamic State. In any case they displayed a soothing routine. The group ate without a lot of appetite and were soon ready to go. Chris felt oddly calm, as if he were about to go hiking with his friends. »I have prepared a bag pack with some food and some other stuff inside.« Paulsen took it and they said goodby to Samara. The host accompanied them to their vehicle. »I was curious what kind of car you were referring to and it is really quite inconspicuous. Just the kind of car the poor people have in this rural region.« The three men disappeared under the tarp and Elena sat next to the host who started the car.

»That reminds me of the day when I brought my niece Ronja to the military base, after she had finished the training.«, he indulged in reminiscences. »She was so proud to be a fighter of the YPG, and was eager to defend her country and her people.« They passed the center of the town which was not too crowded at this time. The only people were clad in black and had weapons. »And despite she sacrificed her life, the enemy is right here in our town«, he murmured gloomily. Elena wanted to say something along the lines that Ronja didn't die in vain and that he could be proud of his niece. But she knew how hollow these words were to someone who lost a loved one. So she said nothing. Instead she said. »I promise, if we make it out of here, we will do anything possible to gather international help for the Kurds.« She suddenly paused as they were driving towards a checkpoint at the town exit, where Islamic state fighters were stopping cars. Her heart began racing. »The host slowed down and casually greeted the fighter. He seemed to know them. He got out of the car and accompanied one fighter to the little hut. What was this all about? After 5 minutes the host came back. »It's alright, we can pass. He set the car in motion while Elene eyed him suspiciously. »What have you told them? What was that?« The host noticed her scepticism. »That was my contact, I paid him and it was not cheap. We were lucky he is still at this outpost.« He stroked her shoulder like a father. »Trust me, you have to calm down. You have a long hike before you.« Elena couldn't calm down though. The closer they came to the mountains the faster her heart seemed to beat. They rode a small road along the course of the river. Everything reminded her of the terrible tragedy of her family. She felt like panicking. »Elena, are you ok? You look pale.« The host asked concerned. Elena didn't answer, instead she grasped the door handle even tighter. The host raised his voice. »Elena listen. I'm gonna tell you a story about my niece Ronja. I once asked her if she was afraid if she lay in the fire trench and the bullets were flying around her neck. Every moment can be your last and you witness terrible things around you. You know what she replied?« Elena shook her head. »She said in these moments she solely focuses on her breath. When inhaling the stomach lifts and when exhaling it becomes flat. That's all, redirecting your attention at your breathing. It's sounds easy, but it works. Do you want to try it out, Elena?« Elana breathed in long into her stomach and exhaled tip her stomach was flat. She focused solely on breathing. After only a few moments she noticed that the panic was settling and her heartbeat was normalizing. She looked at the host gratefully. He gave her a sense of security. She didn't want him to leave them alone.

They had reached the spot where the car couldn't go any further. The host left the road and parked the car behind a row of trees. »From here you have to hike.« It was time to say goodbye to their dear friend, and they reluctantly watched him until he disappeared behind the corner of the road. From now on they were on their own again.

Jed Collins stepped on the gas to get to his team. It was 2 o'clock at night and that meant in Iraq it was 7 o'clock in the morning. And over there they needed his help to catch the prisoners. He passed the last crossing, then he reached the installation. On the vast area where a dozen container standing side by side. From here the drones in the middle east were remote controlled. He parked his car in front of the last container in the row and hurried inside. The interior looked like the cockpit of an airplane. Without windows. The pilots were sitting in front of screens, measurement devices, keyboards, buttons and a joystick. Like in areal plane. »Hallo Sir«, the pilot greeted Jed Collins. Next to him was the co-pilot and sensor operator, operating cameras and radar. »Hey Daniel. Hi Tom.« Jed Collins took a seat behind them for the analysts and looked on his screen. »Is the reaper already in the air?« »Yes Sir, what is our target?« »Our target are 3 or 4 persons trying to escape over the mountains into Iran. You have a map?« Daniel clicked on the map, so they could see the mountains bordering Iran. »Ok let's go to work.«

Chapter 28

By sunny weather and fresh temperatures the hiking group set in motion. They soon reached the timber line and the mountain mass extended before them. Point of orientation was the creek that at times flew down with strength or calm- ly bubbled at others.   The serpentine paths meandering up th mountain were not secured and the abyss was a constant companion. After two hours they took a break on a shadowy spot where the creek was quiet. Chris grabbed a bottle of wa- ter out the backpack and took a long sip before passing it on. Inspecting the inside of the backpack closer he shouted out in surprise. »Look at this. Our friends thought of everything!« He pulled out binoculars, a climbing robe and a big knife and showing it to his companions. »Excellent«, Paulsen replied satisfied studying the map. In the upper part there is a big plane we have to cross where we are quite ex- posed. We will need the binoculars.

They moved on and shortly after reached a slushy snow field they needed to cross. As they were on the northern side of the mountain there were ice plates hidden under the snow. Chris was the first to learn it the hard way. He slipped, fell on the ground and slid down a few yards. It took a moment until he recovered from the impact groaning like an old man. Paulsen helped him up. He pulled out the climbing robe and robed up the group so that they walked in a chain.

Determined they trudged in the footsteps of Paulsen leading the group. Like a caterpillar. Suddenly Elena walking at the end of the chain gave a piercing shriek. The men turned around alarmed. »Look at this.« She indicated at a spot on the edge of the slope about 9 feet next to them where a cadaver of an animal was lying. »That looks terrifying«, Elena said. »What is that?« At first glance it looked like a goat but with a powerful bite and long teeth like a wolf and huge claws. They had goosebumps. »Let's move on.« Paulsen decided. At greater speed than before they marched on.

An hour later they reached the high plateau that was covered with green, juicy meadows. The were stunned by the beautiful panorama. To the left stuck up a steep rock face and the plane ridge extended until the crest. Koletzki peered through the binoculars. »It's all quiet«, he said. »But I have a feeling we better be alert. This looks suspicious.« Chris looked over the plane. »So we have to walk through the plateau and over the ridge and on the other side is Kurdistan?« »That's correct.« Paulsen replied pensively. »But we are on a silver platter here.« He pulled put his camouflage bandana and put it around his head. The others did the same thing. »In order to be invisible, we have to spread wide. Let's walk in the shape of a diamond.« Paulsen in the front and Koletzki in the back with about 30 feet space between them. With his Kalashnikov in hand, Paulsen and his friends roamed the high grass like a pack of pumas. Every no and then Paulsen peered through his binoculars looking for enemy movement.

Suddenly his breath rattled. In the upper third of the ridge he had noticed a slight movement. He gazed more closely and discovered an enemy position. Clicked with his tongue twice he made the sign for attention. When the three had eye contact with Paulsen he indicated the enemy position to them. With naked eye they could only speculate where it exactly was. But there was no other way across the ridge. Now it was kill or be killed. They had to get away from the plateau as fast as possible. About 30 meters in front of them he discovered a ledge about the waist high but in the right angle to the enemy position. Paulsen indicated in military sign language that Elena and Koletzki take cover there and distract the enemy while Chris and himself would walk up on either side to attack the enemy from behind. They had to take advantage of the surprise moment. Looking at one another they nodded. Elena started to creep to the edge of the high grass. She waited a moment and then jumped up and sprinted in a crouched position towards the ledge whirling up dust and pebbles. Everything kept quiet. No shots fired. Now it was Koletzki's turn. He knew that the enemy was expecting him. As soon as he jumped out of the grass onto the track of debris the first shot was fired scraping past him. Under a rain of shots he ran zig zag and with a courageous jump made to the ledge. »Are you hurt?« Elena asked worried looking at his arm. Koletzki realized that a bullet hat scratched his arm. »It's not that bad. We deal with it later. Now we have to distract them.« He took his kalashnikov and aimed at the enemy position diagonally to his left about 20 meters above them unleashing a volley of shots. Elena caught a glimpse of Paulsen roaming through the grass. Then she entrenched herself aiming with her gun at the enemy position and fired. The shots bounced off at the rock making a deafening noise.

In the meantime Chris had climbed up about 20 meters above the ledge on the far left side. The surface was rugged with big rocks giving him cover, so that he could advance fast. His friends needed his help, before they ran out of ammo. Soon he reached a spot where he could peek into the enemy position. He waited a moment taking a breath until his heartbeat recovered. He needed a calm hand. The enemy position was sealed off with big rocks at the sides and canopied with a stone covered tarp. Only the muzzles of the Kalashnikovs were peeking out. Impossible to recognize from the distance with the naked eye. He climbed a little higher, unlocked his gun and waited for Paulsen on the other side. Suddenly a person came crawling out of the enemy position in his direction. His hands clasped the gun. He had never shot at a person, but it was either him or the enemy now. He hoped Paulsen was also ready to attack.

With trembling hands he aimed at the fighter 5 m from him and waited until his head reappeared behind the rock. Then he pressed the trigger. BANG. The sound of the shot echoed like a cannon shot. The body of the fighter crouched and his torn open eyes looked at Chris in surprise until he fell down the steep slope. He had killed a man. But he brushed off the thought, he had to seize the moment of surprise. His shot was the signal to start the attack. He saw Paulsen appear at a higher position with his kalashnikov firing furiously at the enemy position. The enemies were clearly caught by surprise and didn't know from where they were shot at. One enemy fighter peered out of the lookout and was instantly shredded by a volley of shots slumping like a sack of flour. Now there was only one fighter left. Chris had run out of bullets though. The fighter shot his RPG at Paulsen, who ducked low behind the rocks. He saw the wide back of the fighter before him. He pulled out the knife and crept up to the enemy position. Without thinking he jumped behind the fighter and rammed the long knife deep into his flesh. The fighter slowly turned around like he had gotten a shower with an ice bucket. Then he slowly went kneeled down. With his last energy he pulled out his gun and raised it at Chris. But instead of running for cover Chris was like paralyzed in this moment. He knew he had to get out of the shot line, but he couldn't move. He was hypnotized by the dark enemy eyes that glared at him through the slit of the scarf. The Fighter raised his hand and Chris closed his eyes. BANG.

When he opened the eyes, the fighter lay on the ground motionless. Paulsen stood behind him with his gun in hand. »Are you ok?«, he asked Chris and walked towards him. Still in shock he kept glaring at the body on the ground. »These eyes were hypnotizing me«, he stammered with a trembling voice. »I know these eyes.« He walked over to the dead body and pulled the scarf from the head. »It's Lazy Eyes!«, he shouted out in disbelief. The adrenalin still ran through his veins. »Ok, calm down.« Paulsen indicated to Elena and Koletzki to catch up with them. When they arrived they hugged one another ingrate joy. »Good work. All of you.« Paulsen praised them but kept tlooking through his binoculars for more enemies. Elena pulled out the bandages and treated Koletzki's arm wound. Meanwhile Chris enjoyed the view over the green plateau. Incredible that they were able to conquer this enemy position. He looked at the blue sky and the remaining distance to the other side of the crest. He was filled with joyful anticipation when he suddenly saw a sparkling object in the sky.

»There is something on the ridge, Sir.« Jed Collins had received a message by Lazy Eyes of the exact location. The reaper lowered to 12.000 m. The green plateau appeared on their monitor. »Pan the camera to the ridge. Closer.« The co-pilot zoomed in and saw a lifeless body lying on the slope. »That is one of our fighters. But they have to be close.« The pilot exposed the red button and was ready for the commando. The reaper had enough explosives on board to annihilate a little village.

»Look, the Americans!« Chris pointed into the blue sky, where they could make out the drone like a dolphin in the water. But Paulsen tore him back to the ground yelling: »Watch out! Take cover!« He jumped into the trench tearing Chris with him who looked bewildered. »The Americans like to shoot first and ask questions later«, Paulsen explained. They sat in the trench carefully gazing out. Paulsen pulled out his phone and called his special number that has been of help for many times. »Hallo, we are in the Sindshar Mountains bordering Iran. Above us is a drone. Is it from the Americans?« The operator seemed to ask somebody. After a minute he came back. »Negative. The Americans deny having a drone in that area.« They looked incredulously at Paulsen who couldn't believe what he had just heard. »What does that mean?« Paulsen asked. »The Islamic State has a drone?« » I don't know, Sir. All I can confirm is that it is not a drone of the allies. I'm sorry.« Paulsen hung up and looked at the sky with a worried expression who was circling above them. Everybody waited for Paulsen to say something. »We have to find out if they are hostile or friendly towards us.« Paulsen looked at his friends. »I will catch their attention. As soon as they are focused on me, you have to run up and over the crest.« He took a long sip of water, while the rest was in shock. »And what if they shoot at you?« Chris also came to understand what he had just said. »We can just stay here and wait until they fly away.« Paulsen shook his head. »They have probably seen the corpses already. They might

184

even have heat cameras. We don't have a lot of time. No let's go.« He crawled over the dead body of Lazy Eyes. Koletzki held him on the shoulder. »Paulsen, hold on. You don't have to do this. We all know they only want me. Let me go and they will let you go.« Elena looked at him in shock. But Paulsen took his hand. »It is my assignment to get you out of here. And in 25 years I always completed my assignments. It is for the greater good.« He pulled out the letter by the host and gave it to Koletzki. »Promise to fight the Islamic State and those people who support them.« They looked at each other and hugged one another. Then he looked at Chris who was overwhelmed with the emotions. »Chris, you have a good heart. I never thought I would grow fond of you.« He gave him a hug. »If I don't come back, tell my wife and my kids, that I'm sorry.« Chris didn't want to let go of him and looked at him uncomprehendingly. Paulsen wished them good luck and gazed at the sky. The drone circulated above them like a hungry eagle. With a jerk he jumped out towards the rocks that covered him from sight. He tried to bring as much distance between himself and his friends.

Chapter 29

Caro returned with two patient gowns in hand which Adriana pulled over Ibrahim and herself. She tried to put him on his feet - and it worked. His tremor had subsided and so that he would be able to walk slowly. In the meantime some other patients had woken up and looked curiously at the new guests. Adriana adressed Caro, yet raising her voice so that everybody could hear her. »I know you are afraid of fire balls, but do you want to know how a fire ball can't do you any harm?« Bro nodded excitedly. Adriana grabbed a pillow and pushed it against her face so that only her eyes could be seen. »Does everybody see that? The pillow has to be above mouth and nose.« She went through the beds and made some adjustments. When everybody had the pillow before his face she all of a sudden set a handkerchief on fire and then a blanket. Caro ran around panicking and infected the others with it. But Adriana kept the door shut and reminded them to hold the pillows over their faces. When the alarms went off, she opened the door. »Come on everybody, fire! We have to get out of here!« Within seconds mayhem broke loose. The psychiatric patients yelled in panic, started to cry, laughed histerically or even sang and danced. But Adriana shooed them out of the room. The fire had extended on the other sheets and thick smoke moved into the aisle. »Caro you have to warn the other patients in the rooms. And show them the technique!« Adriana ordered.

Chubbs was in his room trying to find some sleep. Although he had taken the sleeping aid, he had woken up again. The program was exhausting and of the 20 men 4 had already checked out. But he wanted to persevere and use the chance, the professor had given him.

Suddenly the door opened and a small woman with pillow in front of her face jumped in. »Fire, Fire, everybody out!« She yelled. »Everybody take a pillow like this and the fire balls will not hurt you!«

The patients flocked down the aisle towards the exit following Caro leading them to the emergency exit. The smoke had become so thick that you could barely see your neighbor. They were about 60 people flushing through the aisle like a wave. Adriana and Ibrahim were in the middle of the crowd. From the corner of her eye she could see the guards and the guy from the nightshift trying to block the way to the emergency exit. But the mass of people was unstoppable. They would have been trampled if they had not dodged. And with everybody holding the pillow over his face it was impossible to recognize them. They passed the guards and climbed up the stairs. With the fire in the back and panic in the bones everybody made it up the stairs. Caro reached the entrance to the first floor first. Exhausted she lay down on the floor like a marathon runner. The night guards hurried to check the people. But in the jostle they didn't notice Adriana and

Ibrahim setting themselves apart and leaving through the side exit. She reached the car of the professor and sat on the driver's seat. Before she started the engine she called 911. »A fire broke out in the basement of the Devereux Colorado. And send police!« She put the folders and documents in the back of the car and started the car.

Paulsen ran, jumped and sliced downhill. His only chance was to run as fast as possible. Although he had scraped his knees and hands bloody he didn't feel pain. His only thought was: run. He made it to the plateaux and sprinted through the green grass. Everything in his body was red alert. The adrenalin numbed the pain and let him rise above his limits. He ran until he had no air left in his lungs and exhaustedly collapsed. Panting for air he lay down in the high grass. His head was spinning and so was the drone above him. The distance to his friends was 400 m. »That should be enough«, he thought. He took a moment to catch his breath and sort his thoughts.

His superiors of the secret service had briefed him, why Koletzki was such an important asset. He knew all about the organization and the highest echelons of the Islamic State. And Paulsen would complete his mission like he always did. He had lived for his job and he would die for it. That was, what he had signed up for.

He thought of his wife and children. The little ones were 4 and 6 years old. It broke his heart, that he would never get to give them a hug, and never laugh or play with them again. He was superman for them, who told them about his adventures saving the world. He hoped they would remember him like this. And his beloved wife. They had got to know in college and she was his one and only love. A love he would have never imagined. He felt grateful to have had such a beautiful wife and mother of his kids. But now she would be on her own. He wiped a tear away and made a cross. He breathed in deeply and looked up. The blue of the sky seemed glaring to him and the little clouds seemed like fluffy sofas gliding on a conveyor belt. He smelled the juicy green grass that mixing with the scent of violets. He became aware of the rustling of the wind, the buzzing of the bees and the ripple of the distant creek. If this was the last moment in his life, it was a nice one. He got up and waved his hands like someone seeking help.

Chapter 30

Jed Collins looked nervously at the screen. »If we don't discover them, we wipe out the area where the dead fighter is laying«, he raged. But suddenly they noticed a movement on the plateau. »Zoom in!« Jed Collins yelled. There was an middle aged man waving a white shirt. He coudlnt see if there were more than one person in the high grass. »Sir? What is your command?«, the pilot asked.

»J-DAM 1000 Kg!«, Jed Collins yelled. The pilot market the target and pressed the red button. »Fire.«

Dropped from the drone the J-DAM is hurtling toward its target at 300 mph. The 14-foot steel bomb uses small gears in its fins to pinpoint its path based on satellite data received by a small antenna and fed into a computer. Just before impact, a fusing device triggers a chemical reaction causing the 14- inch-wide weapon to swell to twice its size. The steel casing shatters, shooting forth 1,000 pounds of white-hot fragments traveling at speeds of 6,000 feet per second. The explosion creates a shock wave exerting thousands of pounds of pressure per square inch (psi). By comparison, a shock wave of 12 psi will knock a person down; and the injury threshold is 15 pounds psi. The pressure from the explosion of a device such as the Mark-84 JDAM can rupture lungs, burst sinus cavities and tear off limbs hundreds of feet from the blast site. When it hits, the JDAM generates an 8,500-degree fireball, gouges a 20-foot crater as it displaces 10,000 pounds of dirt and rock and generates enough wind to knock down walls blocks away and hurl metal fragments a mile or more. «There is a very great concussive effect. Damage to any human beings in the vicinity are pretty nasty. A 2,000-pound bomb has an effective damage radius of hundreds of meters. The 1,000kg Mark 84 Joint Direct Attack Munition (J-DAM) generates a massive fireball and shockwave which also unleashes nearly 500kg of superheated steel fragments, killing anyone within 120 meters and causing injuries out to 1,000 meters.

»Paulsen, no!!« At the spot were Paulsen had waved a moment ago, there was now a black cloud of smoke rising up. Chris had watched Paulsen descending the slope like a maniac. He had hoped until the last moment that the drone was a friendly drone recognizing a refugee. Finally he had watched Paulsen get up and wave. After three seconds of hope everything in the vicinity was torn apart by the gigantic blast. The whole mountain shook rubble and debris rolled down the slope like an avalanche. »Paulsen?« Chris murmured incredulously. Koletzki grabbed him by his shoulders jolting him awake. »We have to get going now or Paulsen died in vain! These are our enemies.« He pointed at the sky. Chris was in shock, but he tried to focus on Koletzki's words. Where the drone was a moment ago, there was now this

191

huge cloud raining pebbles and stones. They were only protected by their scarves but they had to use the moment of in-
visibility. »Come!« Koletzki grabbed Elena by her hand and
started climbing up the slope. It was about 40m to the crest,
but the dust burnt in the eyes and every step was slippery
and dangerous. On all fours the slowly advanced upwards.
Koletzki noticed that the cloud was evaporating and the blue
of the sky became visible again, presenting them to the drone. »Let's fan out.« He yelled. They spread so that there was
a gap of 10 meters between them. With bloody hands Chris
made it to the crest. Carefully he looked over the edge on the
other side. On the south side there were more opportunities
to hide. There were green bushes all over the place. Koletzki
indicated to his friends to fan out more and seek cover behind one of the bushes. They did as told and waited while
the drone was hovering over them.

Ortega raced over the deserted street at breakneck speed until Chad indicated to go slower. »It's on the right.« Ortega
steered the car headed towards a barrier behind which they
could see the area with the containers. »What is this?«, Ortega asked bewildered. He stopped at the cabin next to the
barrier, where a soldier was sitting. Besides him no other
person could be seen. Chad indicated to his friend that it
was his turn to handle the soldier. He grabbed the taser and
walked over to the cabin. »Hey buddy, do you have a lighter

for me?« He showed him his cigarette. »Sure, I got one.«
The young man came out of his cabin and gave Ortega the
lighter. »What is in these containers again?«, he asked the
soldier casually while lighting up. »That's drones.« The soldier looked at him suspiciously. »Are you a soldier at all?«
Ortega pulled out his taser and shot. With a suppressed
moan the soldier fell to the ground and winced with pain.
Before he realized what was happening, Ortega punched him
in the head and sent him straight to wonderland. Chad came
out of the car and fettered the soldier. »That was shack attack!«, he whispered exuberantly. The two partners had fun
together , almost like in the good old days. Chad loaded his
gun and they moved on towards the container. Only the last
container light was illuminated. They crept up. There was
only one strategy for this scenario: stick up.

When the cloud of dust had settled, Jed Collins and the pilots kept looking. He was a meticulous man and didn't want
to run the risk of making a mistake. The drone circulated
above the crest. »Zoom in right there.« Jed Collins had discovered the trench, which was deserted now. »Sir, they
might have crossed the crest and are on the other side.« The
co-pilot suggested. »Alright, let's look on the other side.«
Jed Collins agreed. He was aware of the consequences in
case an American drone shot kurds or refugees on the kur-
dish/iranian territory. But he had no other choice. And acci-

dents happen all the time. It would be a side note compared to the importance of the matter. And that matter was eliminating Koletzki. »There, in the bushes«, the co-pilot pointed at the screen. He zoomed in and there was Koletzki. Beads of sweat were dripping down his forehead and he seemed to look directly at Jed Collins. »Sir, what is your command?« The pilot asked. »Not yet, I want to look at him from up close, before he switched off his light. He had worked with Koletzki for some time. He was the predecessor of Abu Lot as media chief. The German fighters played an important role within the Islamic State. They did a great job off recruiting these young skilled people over there. Koletzki was a journalist but was soon turned by the group dynamic. They had given him a second chance and he had proved his talent. He quickly became an asset and made it to the higher echelons. He even made it into The Big Five, that was the name of the meetings where they shaped the future of the Islamic State. He had liked the German and he felt a little sad, as he watched him crouch in the dirt and sweating from fear. But the business was more important than friendship. He watched the face of his former friend. A last time.

Boom! Chad pushed open the door and burst in. »Nobody moves or I shoot!« He aimed his gun at Jed Collins. Ortega kept the pilots in check. From the edge of his eyes Chad saw the face of a man on the screen. He had a long beard and seemed to be anxiously hiding in some bushes. Then he looked at the pilot and saw the red button before him. He understood what was about to happen. »Slowly put your hands behind your head. Make a move and I will shoot you.« He pushed the barrel at his temples. »Now stand up slowly and go in the back.« The man did as ordered, sitting next to Jed Collins, while Ortega looked turned to the co-pilot. Jed Collins looked at the intruders dumbfounded. He recognized one of them from the bar. But now they wore army uniforms. He didn't know who they were or who they worked for. But he tried to use his authority. »You make a big mistake. This man is a dangerous Islamic State terrorist. We have been looking for him for days. This is a matter of national security.« Chad looked over to the screen »Ah that's the man? He looks like a refugee to me. And by the way, Jed Collins. We know about your dealings with professor Fitzek. And how you ,prepared' Zaidi. You can tell all that to the prosecutor.« Jed Collins gave an imperceptible sign to the co-pilot who was still sitting next to the red button. In a split second he extended his arm and reached for the red button. But with the slightest movement Ortega shot him in his shoulder. He was thrown against the dashboard by the impact and yelled out in shock. »The drone will crash!« Jed Collin yelled. »Shut up.« Chad slapped him in the face. They handcuffed the pilots in the back of the container and fixed them to the chair. Them Ortega took the joystick and maneuvered it around. On the screen he could see an area deserted area. He directed the drone in towards that area with its nose down. Then they grabbed Jed Collins and left for the car. »Get in Mr. Collins. Say goodbye to Fort Carson.«

Chris had moved to the right of the slope where he had discovered a little cave in the rocks. From there he gazed at the sky where the drone was circulating over their heads. He tried to spot his friends on the slope but there were too many obstacles in the way. In his thoughts he was with Paulsen. He knew that it was an enemy drone. But Abu Masala had told them only the Americans had drones. It didn't make sense. Was there a way to capture a drone? Or why would the Americans target them? A movement in the sky tore him out of his contemplation. The drone leaned to the side and made changed his direction. The nose turned towards the ground and it gained speed in an increasingly rapid descend. Chris got up out of his hide-out and gazed at the sky incredulously. The drone was caming down like a drunken eagle.

Chapter 31

»Ahhhhh.« He held his face against the warm water jet and wanted to be one with the water and coat away through the drain. For more than half an hour Ibrahim was taking a shower now in Adriana's hotel room staying to scrub away the bad memories from his soul. Adriana had not reached Ortega and therefore had called Jake to keep her company. After all she didn't know how far the brain of the young man was already damaged and if he was a danger or not. She certainly didn't want to be alone in a room with him. But she wanted to wait for Ortega and Chad before they called the police.

»In the chaos they forgot about the other program. And only after 3 hours they freed the professor from the tube.« Jake recounted. »Apparently the other guy in the room had given him a bad beating. He looked pretty bad when he was carried out.« At the best of Adriana he had driven to the facility to cover the aftermath of the fire along with the journalists. »What will happen to him?« Jake asked. »I hope he will rot in prison for the rest of his life.« Adriana shot back in disgust. For a moment she felt that anger creeping up again, but she wouldn't give in to her emotions now. The knock on the door brought her back into the present moment. The room service had arrived with a big tray covered by a huge bell. They set the table for Ibrahim and called him. Some moments later the young man dressed in a bathrobe dragged himself to the table like a boxer after a fight. Intrigued watched him gorge his food uttering satisfied grunts. Jake whispered to Adriana. »He is eating like an animal. Didn't they give him food all this time?« Adriana scowled at him. »He had been in the tube for 10 days, so I guess that is why.« When he was finished eating she helped Ibrahim on the couch and helped him stretch out his legs. His eyes were still paralyzed and he kept rocking forth and back in his rhythm. »Hallo I am Adriana and this is Jake. Can you tell me your name?« Adriana asked him. Ibrahim looked at her and opened his lips but no articulate words came out. Just a babbling like a heroin junkie. She changed to Yes and No questions. »Your name is Ibrahim?« He nodded. »Can you remember what happened to you?« He nodded again. »Professor Fitzek and his people will be punished for what they did to you and others.« He nodded and took a deep breath. Then she pulled out her phone and dialed the number of his family which Woody from the Miami police department had found out for her. When she heard it ring she gave the phone to Ibrahim. A moment later a distraught voice of a mother was heard. »Hallo? Ibrahim? Is that you?« The fixed gaze of Ibrahim relaxed. He wanted to tell her that he was alive and that he loved her and wanted to hug her and a lot more. But all he managed to say was: »Mama.« »Oh my god it's him!«, his mother cried. »It's alright, Adriana told us where you are. You don't have to say anything now. All we need to know is that you are alive and you will be with us soon.« Overwhelmed she broke into tears and couldn't speak any longer. A rustling sound was heard as the phone was being passed on. Then his father's voice was heard. »Ibo? Ibo my son! I always knew that you are alive.« He also fought the tears. »But everything will be alright now. Inshallah.«

The crash site of the drone was at the opposite slope, about 6 km from them. Chris had witnessed the inferno from his safe hide out. The cloud of dust and pebbles was huge and let it rain even more than before so that he withdrew in the cave. It took more than 10 minutes until the cloud vanished and they could grasp the extent of the explosion. It was detonated on the stoney face of the opposite slope and the blast had left a huge crater in the mountain. Fortunately it had not affected the nearby woods, otherwise there would have been a major inflammation. Chris slowly realized that they had made it. He felt a boundless relief. Waving to his friends he crawled out of his hide outs and signaled to his friends to meet down below. A few minutes later they met in the middle of the slope and hugged one another. »Can you believe that?« Elena asked incredulously. »The drone came down just like that.« They told about their hide outs and how they witnessed the explosion. But the mood was still dim, after the death of Paulsen. Before they kept descending

Koletzki warned them. »Don't forget the Kurds.We are not at home yet.«

With a mix of relief and sadness they marched on. The sun dyed the landscape in a vital green and Chris could peek deep into the green valley. Soon he felt pure joy at the thought of having a Shish Kebab and a whiskey Cola. After 40 minutes they took a rest at a wellspring. »We made it.« He laughed and hugged Koletzki, who was also visibly relieved. »Yes, I think we have made it.« While they talked about their favorite dishes they wanted to have, they suddenly heard a rustle in the bushes. They turned around and looked into the mouths of machine guns of 5 Kurdish fighters. 3 women and two men. With loud yells they ordered them to lay down their weapons and get on the ground. After they had been checked Koletzki succeeded in handing them the letter of their host. The leader of the group read it carefully and indicated her fighters to lower the weapons. »My friends, you are now in safety with us. Welcome to the autonomous country of Kurdistan.« They got up and greeted one another cordially. »We heard the explosion and thought the Islamists had shot down the drone. That's why we thought…« She smiled. »Let's go home and get you something to eat.« The leader said and they marched down. After a while a young female soldier caught up with Chris. »You have a prominent friend who vouched for you.« Chris turned to her in surprise. »You referring to the host?« The soldier laughed. »He is in fact a high ranked commander of the YPG running clandestine operation against the enemy. His name is Mama Risha. A war hero for the Kurds.« She laughed and winked at her comrades. Now he connected the dots. That's why the host was so well organized. And why he was admired for his courage. He also risked his life for them. »Long live mama Risha!« Chris yelled and the soldiers laughed. They hiked down in the high sun tdelighted with the fertile landscape. To Chris it seemed more colorful and magnificent than anything he had seen before.

Chapter 32

We are here in the Devereux psychiatric treatment center in Colorado Springs, where events were overturnt tonight.« The reporter was in the main entrance of the building. »The firemen department was informed of a fire in the basement by an anonymous caller. What the firmen and police found, left them amazed.« The pictures of the control room and the tubes. »They discovered a secret program whose purpose it was - according an analyst - to manipulate suitable minds in order to get them to do crimes in the name of Islam. If it is true, what this analyst is hinting at, it would be a scandal of unfathomed scale. Also the Black Jack killer took purportedly part in this very program.« The camera swiveled to the left and showed Caro and the rest of the patients. »About 60 people were liberated and will be transferred to another institution where they will be checked for damages to the brain.« Then the professor was shown being carried out on a stretcher. »The responsible person of this institution was beaten up by a subject of his. How exactly he ended up in the room with that guy alone is not certified yet. »That was Michelle Lazar, Fox News.«

Ortega gave Adriana a hug and kissed her. Altogether they sat in the hotel room and watched the news. On almost all local channels they reported on the crazy professor and his secret lab. Ibrahim's condition had improved but he kept looking anxiously at the man in handcuffs.

Ortega and Chad had brought Jed Collins with them. Chad had another plan with him than surrendering to the police. »With all the clandestine services with their own budgets you don't know who to trust anymore.« Chad argued. »I mean, what we have seen on that army base in Fort Carson is outrageous. If it hits the news, it's another banger. But these things exist in our country. So how do we know? I'm just an ordinary policeman. It might be that this drone program is approved by some politicians and as soon as he gets his trial they release him and he continues to kill people.« He looked at Jed Collins in disgust. »All I'm saying is this. We have him right here, we know what he is capable of and we can take him out.« Adriana looked at Ortega frowning at him. »You know you could lose your job over this? And worse.« Ortega nodded pensively, then said. »I think Chad is right. We should seize the moment and do what is right. This man is a threat to the public. It feels right to me.« Adriana shrugged her shoulder. »Alright, let's take things in our own hands.« Chad released Jed Collins from his handcuffs. »You're making a big mistake.« As soon as he had opened his mouth, Chad slapped him hard in the face. »You talk, when I tell you to do so. Is that clear?« The emotions were high and Ortega pushed his friend aside and took over. »Now look, Jed Collins. I really couldn't care less about you. But you have a choice. We either put you in a room with

Chad and he will make sure that you will never be able to hurt anyone again.« He paused and looked at Chad. »Or you work with us and help us to gather a meeting of the BIG FIVE.« Jed Collins winced as Ortega uttered the word. »In this case we leave you to the justice system. It's on you.« The CIA man looked at Chad and Ortega standing over him. »Alright, I help you.« He took out his phone and called the number of Abu Masala and put him on the speakers so that everybody could hear. »Asalaamalaikum Mr. Collins.« »Abu Masala, I heard the prisoners have escaped. This is bad. We need to reorganize. You as part in the Big Five will join us.«

25 minutes from the heart of Qatar's vibrant capital, a private helicopter pad offered an exclusive arrival with a bird's eye coastal view at the breathtaking island called banana island. Sheikh al Walid was enticed by the view from the helicopter window. The island extended over 12 ha where a giant hotel complex with all possible amenities awaited the guests. The meeting point was at the tip of the banana where Jed Collins had ordered them. When he entered the maledive style villa, Miller greeted him cordially introducing the new member of the Big Five. »This is the new media chef of the Islamic State, Abu Masala.« He stood up and reverently shook hands with the Sheikh. It was a big moment for him to meet all these important people that supported the caliphate. »Where is Jed Collins?«, the sheik asked.»He is de-

layed for some minutes.« They sat down and had some ice tea. »We had to suffer some major setbacks.« The sheik said. »Abu Hattab escaped, a drone lost, the program lost. You start thinking if it is worth investing in this Islamic State.« He looked at Abu Masala. »Now, it's true that we are in a critical moment. But as bad as it seems. We are not dead yet. We still have new fighters joining us. Only two days ago we conquered a new city in Iraq.« He rubbed his beard. »We should send out a message to the west and show them, for every blow we pay them back 10 times. For the death of Nasrallah we kill 10 Kufars, for the lost drone we kill 10 Kufars and for the escape of Abu Hattab we kill 10 more.« He felt in his element. The sheikh was satisfied. »Well I see, you haven't lost hope. That is good. Let's see what Jed Collins says.« A few moments later Jed Collins entered the room. Rigidly he walked in the center of the room and looked at his friends. Then he looked down. »I'm sorry.«

In the next moment, hell broke loose. A dozen men with rifles stormed the room from every angle of the villa. Windows shattered and doors were kicked in. And everybody yelled: »On the floor! Don't move!«

Abu Masala remained seated, bewildered and shocked. Now that he had achieved what he had dreamed for so long, it was all over? He saw the angry eyes of the women. They had to be YPG fighters. Adriana had managed to contact Koletzki and told him about their plan. He passed it on to the commander Mama Risha who was willing to send his best men and women.

Abu Masala had heard about the Kurdish prisons and how they treated Islamic State fighters. The mere thought of spending the rest of his life in a Kurdish prison send shivers down his spine. Compared to that Guantanamo was a holistic spa resort. Horrified he shook his head. Unfortunately he didn't wear his suicide belt. But he would go to paradise anyway. He looked at his friends and yelled from the top of his lungs: »Allahu Akbar!« Then he jumped up and lunged at the nearest soldiers. They seemed to have waited for this moment. Instantly let the bullets rain on him and perforated his body. The impact of the bullets hurled him against the wall 3 m behind him. Within seconds his body was shredded like after a shark attack. After the last shot was fired there was dead silence. The sharks looked at the other fish blood thirsty. »Make a move and we will send you to paradise.« But nobody dared to move.

Chapter 33

»During the trial you have heard the testimony of witnesses who were described as experts.

Merely because an expert witness has expressed an opinion does not mean, however, that you must accept this opinion. The same as with any other witness, it is up to you to decide whether you believe this testimony and choose to rely upon it. Part of that decision will depend on your judgment about whether the witness's background or training and experience is sufficient for the witness to give the expert opinion that you heard. You must also decide whether the witness's opinions were based on sound reasons, judgment, and information.

The Court room was filled to the brink. Adriana had stated her expert opinion and now it was on the jury to decide.

Zaidi looked better now. He changed a look with his parents holding hands in the second row. After Adriana's expert opinion there was no doubt that Yusuf was used as a tool and didn't act on his own will. Therefore it didn't make a difference if he shot or a third person was involved. The man behind him was responsible. And that was Jed Collins, who was now put to trial.

The jurors returned from the courtroom.

The audience looked at the foreperson in suspense. »The jury unanimously came to a verdict. The accused was found not guilty«, he announced the verdict.

A cry of joy fulfilled the court room. Yusuf was freed from his handcuffs and stormed into the arms of his parents. Adriana wiped her tears away. Ortega swang his arm around her and drew her close. »You did a great job. You saved the man's life. And many other's as well.« Adriana smiled at him. »I wouldn't have made it without you.« He gave her a kiss. They turned to the freshly reunited family and left them to themselves in their joy.

Chapter 34

Chris rang the bell of his friend's house. It was a warm day in the spring of Berlin and he was looking forward to meeting his friends again. Koletzki opened the door with a big smile on his face and greeted his dear friend. The memory of their adventure was still present in their minds and grew stronger whenever they saw one another. Koletzki had moved to Berlin with Elena as he was working with the secret service in the department of counter terrorism focusing on the Islamic State. »Chris is here!«, he yelled into the corridor and a moment later Elena came running towards him and jumped in his arms. They lead him into the living room. »May I introduce you to a friend of mine?« Chris looked surprised at the sofa where a beautiful woman stood up and greeted him. »That is Kyra. From my department. She speakes Swedish, Arabic, English, German and Spanish.« Kyra laughed embarrassed. »I didn't speak Spanish in a while.« Her smile was breathtaking, so was the rest of her. She was a nordic beauty with blue eyes and blonde hair. Koletzki and Elena changed a telling look and blinked. Chris was obviously pleased. They sat down and drank a glass of wine.

»Elena told me that you were given a medal of honor, is that true?« Her little nordic accent turned her words into music.
»Yes, well the medal of honor was more likely a tribute to our dear friend Paulsen. Without him we wouldn't be here

tonight.« They thought a moment in silence of their dear friend. »I'm sorry I didn't want to bring up bad memories.« She was not only intelligent, but also emphatic. »No it's alright. He deserves to be mentioned and remembered.« Kyra changed to a lighter subject. »What are you doing at the moment?« She asked. »I'm preparing for a documentary on Colombia, my mother's home country.« Kyra smiled at him. She seemed intrigued and attracted. »Medellin.« Chris added with a grin.

Elena pulled Koletzki in the kitchen. »I think she likes him. What are you thinking?« Koletzki chuckled. »Yes, and I think he will mess it up sooner or later«, he laughed. »But that's only a guess.

When they came back Chris and Kyra were sitting on the sofa kissing each other. They stopped embarrassed when they noticed their hosts. Chris got up cheerfully and dragged Koletzki to the balcony for a cigerette. He presented a joint and lit it. »She is really gorgeous. Thanks for introducing, bro.« He took a deep breath and passed it to Koletzki. »What's the situation in Syria and Iraq now. Are we winning?« Koletzki cautiously tasted the joint, then answered. »The Islamic State is losing more and more ground. With the blow against the 'Big Five' we have eradicated the most valuable actors. They desperately struggle to show they are still alive. But the YPG is advancing fast, Mama Risha told me.« Chris inhaled and held his breath. »That's good.« Koletzki nodded. »I recently talked to Ortega and Chad. They told me how they saw me at the screen in that container.« He shook his head. »Chad said, whenever he would go to the bushes during a hike, he will remember my frackled face.« Chris laughed out loud and slapped Koletzki on his shoulder.

When they had finished smoking and reentered the room, Elena seemed to sleep on the couch. Koletzki was about to say something funny, when suddenly Kyra appeared with a gun in her hand. Only now he realized the unnatural position of Elena's head. The Swedish woman gave off two shots with her silenced gun. Blood splashed against the wall. Then she made a call and waited. »Sir, mission is completed.« Well done, Kyra. Come back home«, Jed Collins answered.

Thanks

A big thanks goes out to a person who supported the book project from the beginning. Susanne E. Is the mother of a young jihadist who is still in Syria. Last year she had accompanied me to one of my lectures and about the methods and recruitment of ISIS and recounted her experiences with the jihadists and how they brainwashed her son.

She couldn't understand that these recruiter could run around undisturbed recruiting young men like her son in plain view of the secret agencies. All Protected by freedom of religion.

And she wondered how it's possible, that there are german universities sponsored by Saudi families whose agenda is to promote Wahabism and Salafism, with student exchanges to universities in Alexandria where the young men are pulled deeper into the net of the jihadists.

Her son was located in Raqqa and is said to have a wife and a baby, as she had learnt through some contacts.

It is her biggest dream to meet with her son again.

A last thought

The research on the book lead me deeply into the human psyche. It is sad to see so many young people in a situation so desperate and without perspectives, that they throw away their lives so easily. Best example is the former rapper Deso Dogg, who was a gangster in Berlin, Kreuzberg. He felt mistreated by his record label and found himself a financial crisis, up until the point, where he turned his anger into something more evil.

According to the propaganda of ISIS their aim is a just state, where the people can live acoording to the rules of the Sharia. But the reality is vastly different. Which is no surprise if the power is in the hands of those young and unstable individuals like Deso Dogg.

Fortunately the Islamic State will soon be eradicated. But the idea of a just state for the believers will live on.

Visit me on facebook: Matthias Richter

and Soundcloud: Mati Caruso.

We are the resistance!

www.ingramcontent.com/pod-product-compliance
Lightning Source LLC
Chambersburg PA
CBHW020602030726
47497CB00007B/2050